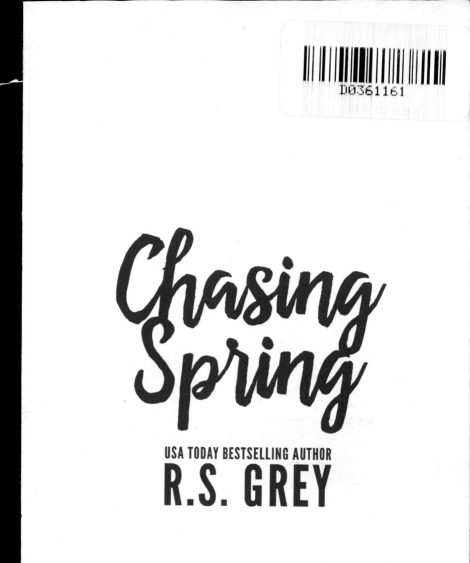

Chasing Spring

USA TODAY BESTSELLING AUTHOR

R.S. GREY

Published: R.S. Grey 2016
authorrsgrey@gmail.com
Editing: Editing by C. Marie
Cover Design: R.S. Grey
Stock Photos courtesy of Shutterstock ®
All rights reserved.
ISBN: 1519536615
ISBN-13: 978-1519536617

R.S. Grey

For my mom.

R.S. Grey

PROLOGUE

I love secrets and I'm good at finding them. For the last two years, I've sat and waited and watched. I've learned to collect secrets one by one because secrets are flames and no place deserves to burn more than my small town.

CHAPTER ONE

Lilah

I WASN'T SUPPOSED to move back to Blackwater, Texas. I'd never agreed to it, but I still stood on the curb of my aunt's apartment complex with my moving boxes stacked up beside me. There were five in total: three for clothes, one for toiletries, and one for books. The only two things I actually cared about—my journal and my lock pick kit— were tucked in the bottom of my backpack, hidden beneath an old sweatshirt.

The edge of the lock pick kit cut into my back as I stood waiting for my dad. I reached back to feel for it just as his old truck rumbled through the gates of my aunt's apartment complex, ready to cart me back home.

Blackwater, Texas - Population: small.

I'd left my hometown before the start of junior year and I'd had every intention of staying in Austin indefinitely. Blackwater held nothing for me. Unfortunately, my aunt's company wanted to transfer her overseas and my dad wouldn't hear of me living by myself for the rest of senior year.

He pulled up in front of the curb, put his truck in park, and hopped out to meet me. The chilly air showed his breath as he brought his hands to his mouth to warm them but he stopped short when he glanced up and saw me.

"Your hair's black," he noted with a tilt of his head. His look betrayed no hint of disapproval. He was just surprised.

"And yours is gray," I countered.

He cracked a smile and whipped off his Blackwater Baseball hat. "It's salt and pepper."

I nodded. "Well mine is just pepper."

I felt for one of my short strands as he stepped forward and engulfed me in a tight kind of hug only dads can give. I resisted for a second before hugging him back.

When he stepped away, I realized he looked a little more worn than when I'd last seen him. He was still handsome in his early forties, but he looked grittier around the edges. The last two years had taken their toll on his warm brown eyes and despite his estimation, I spied more salt than pepper peeking out of the bottom of his hat.

He pointed at my cropped hair. "I see the blonde trying to come back."

Not if I can help it.

We loaded up my boxes in the bed of his truck as he buzzed with excitement. He thought I belonged at home with him. He was wrong. I didn't want to leave Austin, but the idea of uncovering my small town's secrets made it a little easier to slide across the stained cloth seats of my dad's pickup.

I dropped my backpack between my legs, brushed my fingers over the outline of the lock pick kit, and then straightened up to buckle my seatbelt.

"Think we'll have a good spring this year?" he asked, pulling the stubborn gearshift down to put the truck into drive.

What a loaded question.

I offered a wordless shrug. I spent most of my time alone, and veiled small talk was not one of my strong suits.

He took a patient breath. "You know, you're moving back home at the perfect time. I spent all week fixing up those flowerbeds out back. Everything is ready to go when it warms up."

I had loved springtime growing up and he knew it. Flowers bloom, temperatures warm, and sunny days stretch out longer before yielding to the night. Even so, I hadn't loved spring since leaving Blackwater, and fresh flowerbeds wouldn't change that. *Couldn't.*

I kicked off my shoes, brought my knees to my chest, and wrapped my arms around them. I dropped my head to my knees and envisioned the small garden that sat behind our cottage house. Every year like clockwork, my mom and I had sat out there in late January and planned what we would plant for the year. Tomatoes in barrels near the back porch. Lettuce, peppers, squash, and carrots in the first four flowerbeds. Fruit of all kinds usually took up the beds near the fence. From what I remembered, we could never master the fickle raspberry vine.

"Lilah."

I was so entranced by the rich memory of that old garden that I didn't hear my dad speak up until he repeated my name.

"*Lilah.*"

I turned toward him.

"I just wanted to say that I'll give you a hand when it's

time to start planting. And maybe Chase can help out too."

My heart skidded to a stop beneath my white tank top.

"What are you talking about?"

Chase Matthews was the last person I would have expected my dad to bring up in a conversation about my mother's old hobby.

My dad sighed and flicked his warm gaze to me, only taking his eyes off the road for a moment, but shooting me a warning nonetheless. "He's going to be staying with us for the next few months—"

"WHAT?"

"I know that it's going to be an adjustment, but it's just for a little while—'til graduation at the latest."

He finished his sentence as if it would clear up my confusion, but it made no sense.

"Why would he need to? He has a home."

My dad shook his head. "It's complicated, Lilah. You've been away and haven't seen..." He paused, searching for the right words. "Well, Mr. Matthews has been getting worse lately. It's not a good situation for Chase to be in, and it's been a long time coming for him to finally admit it."

I threw up my hands. "So that's it? Chase has an alcoholic dad so he gets to move in with us? I don't get a say?" I hated that I sounded like a whiny brat.

My dad dragged his teeth across his bottom lip before answering. "This is bigger than you, Lilah."

I rolled my eyes. Right. Because I couldn't possibly understand the gravity of the situation. I understood just fine; Chase needed to get out of his house, but that didn't mean he needed to move into ours. Clearly my dad hadn't thought this through.

"Where's he going to stay? It's not like we have an extra room," I pointed out.

He kept his eyes on the road.

"In the bedroom across the hall from you." He answered quickly as if he knew his words would hurt me; he was trying to counteract their effect.

I narrowed my eyes. "That's not a bedroom. That was mom's space."

He sighed. "For all her faults, your mother would have offered that room in a heartbeat."

I shot him a narrowed glance and he countered with a warm smile. "I know you'll come around, Lil. It'll be fine. The kid needs a stable home. I hope you'll welcome him with open arms."

Over my dead body. We might've been friends once, but I'd avoided Chase for the last year and a half. That wasn't about to change just because he was moving in across the hall. If I was forced to be his roommate, I'd be a silent one.

"When is he coming?" I asked, eyeing the chipping blue paint on my nails.

"Tomorrow."

Tomorrow?

I had less than twenty-four hours to Chase-proof my life.

My dad rested a hand on my shoulder. The comforting pressure was supposed to tell me everything would be okay, but I swallowed down a lump of emotion and turned away.

"Y'know Lilah, you should look at this like it's a fresh start. No one wants to dig up the past."

He was wrong.

I did.

CHAPTER TWO

Lilah

MY OBSESSION WITH secrets had started out innocently enough. The window at my aunt's apartment faced the parking lot adjacent to a rundown city park. It was rarely used for recreation; the basketball courts weren't much use without rims, and the tennis court nets looked like the ragged sails on a ghost ship. Instead, during the early hours of the morning, people would park there for two reasons: sex and drugs. More often than not, the hookups outnumbered the drug deals.

I'd watch the drama unfold from the edge of my bed, parting the cheap plastic blinds to get a better view. Their cars would fill with lazy white smoke and their windows would fog over. Their chaotic lives were mesmerizing and I craved the moments in my day when their secrets chased away mine.

I had used some leftover Christmas money on a website

that charged ten dollars in exchange for the name and address registered to a Texas license plate. With seemingly innocuous information, my world of secrets started to spread.

I could lose myself in hours of Google searches, Facebook and Instagram accounts, and public records. They made it all too easy. Then again, someone hooking up in a public park probably isn't too preoccupied with privacy.

Unfortunately, after a few months, that perch on my bed was no longer enough. It was the same couples and the same drug addicts night after night. Their secrets became boring and predictable. That's when I bought a lock pick kit online. I tracked the package incessantly and on the day it was due to arrive, I hurried home from school to intercept it before my aunt got home from work. It'd taken me two nights to read through the manual and two weeks to master the art.

My dad could cart me back to Blackwater, and he could force me to put up with Chase in the bedroom across the hall, but he couldn't take away my obsession. I had two days before school started and I intended to make good use of those forty-eight hours.

• • •

The morning of Chase's impending arrival, I woke up bright and early and threw on jeans, tattered Converse, and an old Blackwater dance team shirt I hadn't seen since moving to Austin. The cotton was worn and soft, the same as when I'd left it.

I stuffed my lock pick kit into my purse and checked that I had a few bobby pins for backup. I walked out into the hallway and locked my bedroom door. The room across the hall beckoned, but I ignored it. The door was closed and for all I knew my dad had already cleared her stuff out and prepared it for Chase's arrival. What did it matter? It wasn't like it belonged to my mother any more anyway.

I turned and headed for the stairs, catching sight of myself in the mirror hanging on the opposite wall. When I'd been younger, my dad would lift me up so I could see my reflection.

In that moment, I saw myself whether I wanted to or not. My fake black hair made my freckles stand out even more against my fair skin, and I liked the effect. I inspected my blonde roots, which were inching out more and more every day; I'd have to do something about them eventually.

My dad was in his room downstairs, but I discovered a sticky note he'd left for me in the kitchen. He'd created a stack of breakfast foods: a box of oatmeal on bottom with a banana balancing on top. The sticky note was stuck to the top of the banana and he'd added a smiley face for emphasis.

Breakfast :)

I could hear the TV in his room replaying baseball footage from years past. I ignored the oatmeal, grabbed the banana, and headed out the door. It was 9:30 AM on a Saturday and I had nowhere to go. My options were limited considering I had no friends in Blackwater; I hadn't kept in touch with anyone. The town had one coffee shop and if I remembered correctly, it was usually overrun by a bridge club on Saturday mornings. I resolved to head in that direction anyway.

I slipped my headphones in and started the short walk toward the town square, hopeful that something would catch my attention on the way. I was at the end of the street—about to turn the corner onto Main Street—when I heard a car rumbling down the road behind me. The distinct sound was loud enough to disrupt my Vance Joy playlist and there was only one car in town that was that decrepit. My gut clenched and I turned despite my better judgment, just in time to see the clunky monster swerve up into our driveway. The truck had seen better days, possibly during the Nixon administration, but Chase owned the wear and tear like a badge of honor. Like most things, the old truck just added to the small town charm of Chase Matthews. All-American baseball star. Prom king. Heartthrob. My ex-best friend.

He was sitting behind the wheel, staring up at my small house. Even from down the street I could make out his handsome profile from behind his truck's dusty windows. He was perfect. The culmination of good genes and baseball practice made it easy for him to fill out his tall frame. I couldn't see his hazel eyes from where I stood, but if I closed my mine, I could imagine them clear as day.

He lingered there for a few minutes, taking in our house. Then his head shifted to the passenger seat, and my heart dropped.

I turned and ran; he couldn't know I was watching him.

I kept running right down Main Street and even as I slowed to a walk, I couldn't brush away the memory of his smile. That was the hardest thing to forget about Chase. It didn't matter that I hadn't seen it up close in a year and a half; it'd been my constant companion for sixteen years.

CHAPTER THREE

Chase

I STARED UP at the Calloways' house and tried to find the courage to get out of my truck. I checked for life behind the living room curtains and the window that ran along the upstairs hallway. I hadn't been inside their house in over a year, and I had no clue what waited for me on the other side of that front door.

I didn't want to move in with the Calloways, but thanks to my dad, I didn't really have a choice. In recent years, he'd progressed from the fun-loving life of the party into a miserable alcoholic that drank alone. A few days earlier, Coach Calloway had stopped by and found him asleep in a pool of his own vomit with the oven left on, and he wouldn't hear of me continuing to live there. So there I was, practically an orphan.

I unbuckled my seatbelt and turned to where Harvey

was sitting next to me on the bench, unabashedly licking his crotch. *Typical dog.* I reached out and scratched the sweet spot behind his ear.

"Should we head in?" I asked the two-year-old golden retriever.

He tilted his head to the left and let his tongue hang out. It was as much of a yes as I'd ever get.

I opened my truck door and hopped out just as the front door swung open. Coach Calloway stepped out with a cup of coffee. He held his free hand up to block the morning sun and nodded a welcome.

"Mornin'. Need help with your stuff?"

I shrugged. "It's not much. I just have a few bags and Harvey's bed."

At the sound of his name, Harvey tried to shove past me so he could jump down and get to Coach Calloway. He pawed at my jeans and when that didn't work, he let out a desperate bark. All in all, it wasn't a stellar first impression.

"We can keep him outside if it'll be trouble. I just couldn't leave him at home. My dad forgets to feed him."

Coach's gaze hit mine. "No trouble at all. Lilah always wanted a dog. She'll be excited."

I glanced behind him at the mention of her name.

"You just missed her though," he continued. "We'll have to introduce her to Harvey later."

I wasn't surprised to find that Lilah wasn't part of my welcoming committee, but a part of me wished she had been waiting for me in the house. I was done playing the silent game. I'd been done the first day she'd started to ignore me, but she'd moved off to Austin and left a gulf between us. Now that she was back, I wondered if her silence would last.

CHAPTER FOUR

Lilah

ADDICTION IS A powerful thing. One hit, one taste of a drug can generate an itch that a lifetime of scratching can't soothe. Contrary to what most afterschool specials preach, the substances themselves aren't powerful boogeymen that ruthlessly conquer the strong wills of stable people. No, they're all just differently colored sparks, and some people are more flammable than others.

My mother was addicted to everything under the sun. Pain pills hoarded from an embellished chronic back injury. Alcohol, a staple from her youth. Meth, a rural infection whose toxic tendrils tore away the shards of her slowly shattering life. Her dependencies occupied the driver's seat for most of my life. After her funeral, I sat in the front of the church as relatives in ill-fitting formal clothes took turns offering some variation of "just know that your mother loved you more than anything". But I knew better; if what they said had been true, she would have still been alive to tell me herself.

I browsed through the aisles of Crosby's Market, trying to stretch out my grocery store run as long as possible. I carried my empty basket down one aisle and then doubled back, confirming the absence of the things I needed. They didn't have places like Whole Foods in Blackwater. There wasn't an organic, gluten-free, vegan, or free-range label in sight. If it wasn't canned or processed, chances were you weren't going to find it at Crosby's. Fortunately, I wasn't there for food.

I strolled down the soap and shampoo aisle, stopping short at a small display of hair dye. They had five colors: black, dark brown, light brown, blonde, and fire engine red. Most of the boxes were expired and the ones that weren't had misshapen packages as if they'd been knocked off the shelf and replaced too many times. I hesitated over the box of blonde hair dye with a smiling woman on the front, and instead reached for the jet-black.

"Wait, don't take that one."

A thin hand reached around my shoulder to grab for a box at the back of the shelf. I turned to find a girl behind me, smiling and holding out the new box for me to take. Her eyes were rimmed with black eyeliner and her blonde hair faded to bright pink halfway down as if she'd dipped the strands into a bucket of radioactive paint that morning. She was tall, with spindly arms and hollow cheekbones.

I took the box and stared down at it. "Thanks."

"Kids always mess with the ones in the front. Usually I get home to find half the stuff missing."

"Makes sense," I said, tossing the new box of hair dye into my basket.

"I'm Ashley," she said, offering a gentle, awkward wave. The name confirmed that I knew her, vaguely. She'd moved to town our freshman year of high school, but I'd never had a reason to talk to her before moving to Austin.

"I'm Lilah."

Her smile faltered at the mention of my name. She hadn't recognized me at first, but as her eyes roamed my features, trying to extract my old persona, I knew it was too late to hope for anonymity.

"You're back?" she asked.

I shrugged. "Looks like it."

I knew why she was confused. I'd left Blackwater as a blonde dance team captain and had returned as a choppy-haired vampire.

After a few moments of her standing there dumbstruck, I stepped past her in pursuit of the cash register.

"Well, see you around."

"Wait," she said, reaching her hand out to stop me. "I don't know what your plans are for the rest of the day, but I'm pretty good with hair dye…"

She let her gaze linger on my blonde roots.

"My house is just down the street," she continued.

Her invitation took me by surprise considering the fact that we'd never been friends. Maybe I had a bright, scrolling marquee across my forehead that read "HELP. I'M IN NEED OF A FRIEND", or perhaps it was the other way around. Either way, if going to Ashley's house delayed the inevitable return to mine, I was in.

• • •

Ashley's house was just a few streets away from mine, close enough that I swore I could hear the rumble of

Chase's truck from my perch in her bathroom. She worked her way through my hair with the dye and I sat on a stool, watching her in the mirror.

"Nothing's changed much since you've been gone."

I raised my eyebrows, curious about what she meant.

"Kimberly and the dance team girls are still popular. Josh Hastings is still the quarterback and he's tied with Trent Bailey for second. It sort of depends on if you prefer jocks or bad boys."

"Second...like, second place?"

Her brown eyes met mine in the mirror. "For hottest guy at school."

In a small town like Blackwater, it was slim pickings when it came to guys. I had forgotten that any girl in school would have been able to spout the most eligible guys in our class off the top of her head.

"I personally think Trent is cuter," she said.

I remembered Trent. He had black hair and perfectly imperfect features. Before I'd left town, he'd already been arrested three times, ranging from small time drug dealing to underage drinking. If Ashley referred to him as a bad boy, chances were he hadn't changed his ways during my time away.

"And you already know who holds the number one spot," she smirked.

Chase.

I bit down on the inside of my cheek. "Can we talk about something else?"

She blushed and ducked her to head to reach for another hair clip.

"Oh, uh, sure."

I'd embarrassed her.

"What are you doing tonight?" I asked.

For one, I wanted her to know that I wasn't going to ditch her after she finished dying my hair; I wasn't in a position to turn down friends. Also, I didn't want to go home.

Her eyes widened with hope. "Actually, there's this party over at—"

"Sounds good," I interrupted, offering her my best attempt at a real smile.

CHAPTER FIVE

Chase

MY DAD HAD inherited a repair shop in the town square from his father, who'd inherited it from my great-grandfather. There was a 1950s sign out front that boasted, "If it's broken, we can fix it." As a kid, I'd learned how to fix everything from toasters to washing machines, but my real forte was repairing vintage cameras. We didn't get many of them in the shop, so few in fact that my dad had always cast them aside to me. It wasn't worth his time to learn how to fix them.

I broke the first four cameras he gave me. They were difficult repairs, but tinkering with them felt like a puzzle, a puzzle with big payouts in the end. Vintage Polaroid cameras went for a hundred dollars, but restored Leicas could go for a couple thousand. Leicas were my specialty.

I still took in cameras from the repair shop, but the

quantity couldn't compare to the ones I found online. I usually spent a couple hours a week searching around online for rare finds, the specialty cameras that hadn't worked in years. Those were the most fun to fix; they taught me that there was value in trying to fix something even when everyone else has given up.

I hopped down from the bed of my truck with a box of vintage cameras in tow. It was the last box of the day and I rested the corner of it against my hip as I closed my lift gate, hoping the pile of rust would stay intact for another day.

Harvey stuck close to me as I walked up the sidewalk and into the house. He'd been confused all day, following me back and forth for each trip to and from my truck. Neither one of us was sure of what to make of our new home.

I pushed opened the door to my room and Harvey ran in first, sniffing the carpet around the bed. It smelled different than our house, a fact he picked up on even more than me.

Coach Calloway had insisted he was giving me a spare room, but I knew that wasn't the case. The stack of boxes with Elaine Calloway's name scribbled across the side of them proved it. This was her room, and I felt like an intruder.

I glanced around, looking for some space to carve out as my own, but the stack of boxes in the corner kept grabbing by attention. I dropped my cameras on the bed and turned toward them. If I was going to be an intruder, I might as well start acting like one.

I pulled the top off the box on top. An empty perfume bottle rattled against the side as I rooted through the contents. It looked like a bunch of junk, but at the very bottom I found a photo of a young Elaine Calloway sitting between her parents. She was the spitting image of them both. Her mom had her arm wrapped tightly around her, leaning over as if shielding her from the world. Her dad wore a sharp expression, his dark brown eyes staring straight into the soul of the person snapping the photo.

Her dad.

The man who'd started it all.

Fucking prick.

I tossed the cardboard lid back onto the box and stood up.

"Let's go, Harvey,"

I slid on my running shoes without untying them, picked up his leash, and flew down the stairs.

CHAPTER SIX

April 1985
Blackwater, Texas

ELAINE CALLOWAY HAD always prayed for a sister, a guardian angel, or a hero. She'd sink to her knees in the back of her family's trailer and clasp her hands together until her knuckles turned white. Her prayers didn't drown out the sound of her father's blows; there was no escaping them in their doublewide, but that didn't keep her from trying.

On particularly bad nights, her mom would sneak into her small bedroom and shove a change of clothes into her backpack for school. On those nights she never let Elaine see her face, hiding behind her long blonde hair, but Elaine knew better. Her mama was the prettiest lady in the whole town and she never covered up her face unless it was black and blue.

"Baby, go to Hannah's house. Sneak out the window and ride your bike to Hannah's." Her pale green eyes pleaded with Elaine to understand.

Elaine glanced down at her pajamas, confused. "Mama, it's a school night. I'm not supposed to be out late on a school—"

"Elaine!" her mom yelled, before softening. "Do what I say, sweetie. Hurry."

Elaine shook, trying to keep from crying. Her mama never yelled, not at her.

"Susan! God dammit, I'm not done talking to you!"

Her mama flinched at the sound of his voice. She bent low and put her face right in front of Elaine's, letting her see the worst of it. Her mom's lip was split open and her left eye was already big and puffy, almost twice the size of the right one.

"Please go," her mom pleaded.

Elaine couldn't stop the tears. She couldn't be a big girl.

"Come with me," Elaine begged. "Come with me to Hannah's!"

Her mom shook her head and moved to the window. She flipped open the rusted lock and pushed it up. A gust of cold night air rushed in and Elaine crossed her arms, trying to keep warm. Her mom tossed her backpack out onto the grass and then turned back for Elaine, waving her closer.

Her dad's heavy steps sounded in the hallway, growing louder as he yelled. His words were nasty and filled with hate. They were the kind of words that earned Elaine a smack on the butt, but there was never anyone around to punish her dad.

He banged on Elaine's door, turning the knob until the cheap particleboard began to splinter.

"Open the door!" he yelled.

Her mom rushed forward and grabbed Elaine's arm, yanking her toward the window.

"Ride your bike to Hannah's," she insisted. "You remember the way. Just like we practiced—"

"OPEN THE DOOR," her dad yelled again, his fist banging and banging and banging.

Her mom lifted her up, trying to get her to climb out the window.

"I don't want to leave," Elaine cried, clinging to her mom's neck. "Please. Come with me. Please come!"

"Go, baby. I'll come get you after school tomorrow. GO."

She pushed Elaine toward the window and held her steady as she climbed through. It was a three-foot drop from the window to the front yard, and when her bare feet hit the soft grass, she looked up and met her mom's pale green eyes.

"I love you," she said just as the thin door gave way to her dad's fists. "GO."

Elaine turned, yanked on her backpack, and ran for her hot pink bike lying on its side in the dirt. She tried to block out the sounds coming from her bedroom as she peddled away. They were the noises that kept her awake at night, the noises that haunted her dreams.

She peddled fast, leaving the rotten trailer park behind to cross over Main Street. Hannah's house was in a better part of town, where the houses had big porches and roses in the front yard. Elaine unlocked the gate on the short fence and dropped her bike in the grass. She tiptoed around the edge of the house until she reached Hannah's window in the back. Her friend was sleeping in her princess bed, under a ceiling painted to look like a blue sky, clouds and all.

"Psst. Hannah," Elaine said, tapping her small finger

against the glass. "Hannah!"

Her friend shot up in bed and squealed when she saw Elaine outside. She scooted out of her blankets and rushed for the window. Her small hands had to work on the lock for a few seconds before she could slide the window up just enough for Elaine to climb through.

She took Elaine's backpack and then helped tug her inside, too excited to notice Elaine's tearstained cheeks.

"I was hoping you'd come tonight!" Hannah said. "My mom gave me cookies after dinner and I snuck an extra one for you."

She turned for her nightstand and pulled out a cookie wrapped tightly in a napkin. She cradled it in her palm as she carried it to Elaine.

It was still warm, and when Elaine bit into it and let the chocolate chips melt on her tongue, she realized that she didn't need to pray for a guardian angel.

She had Hannah.

CHAPTER SEVEN

Lilah

MUSIC POUNDED AROUND us as I followed Ashley through the crowded party, keeping my gaze focused on her back. I wasn't ready for a slew of hometown reunions; my first day back at school was sure to have enough to last me a lifetime.

Ashley bypassed the keg and beer pong tables and led us toward a gazebo in the backyard. There was a small group gathered there and as we stepped closer, I noticed Trent Bailey perched inside.

He glanced up and smiled, and I was momentarily caught in his web. It was easy to see his appeal. He was the kind of cute that no one had expected. He'd somehow broken his ancestors' chain of mediocrity, blending his parents' frumpy genes into an offspring worthy of attention.

He patted the seat beside him in the gazebo, Ashley pushed me forward, and I slid down to claim the bare patch of wood between him and his friend, resisting the urge to wave the cigarette smoke away from my face. The scent of tobacco brought back vivid memories of when I'd lost my virginity. At the start of my junior year in Austin, I'd been approached by a nameless boy. He'd asked me to be his girlfriend, and two months later, he took my virginity in a flash of sweaty limbs, tobacco breath, and scratchy sheets. I'd kept my eyes closed the entire time, and at the end, I'd stared up at the ceiling through the haze of his cigarette smoke and thought of Chase.

Trent Bailey reminded me of that boy back in Austin, with his lit cigarette and his leather boots. He was the same sort of grunge and my stomach rolled as he leaned in to whisper in my ear. "When'd you get back in town?"

"Yesterday."

Trent tossed his cigarette butt on the floor of the gazebo and crushed it beneath his boot. "I like the hair. The black suits you more than the blonde."

I stared down at where the cigarette ash stained the wood, and then the smell of vodka momentarily overpowered the scent of tobacco. It was my turn to sip from the half-empty bottle getting passed around the group. I reached out and accepted it from Trent's friend beside me. The cheap paper label was already soaked from lazy sips, and as I tipped it back to my mouth, I hovered the lip of the bottle so that the clear liquid slipped into my mouth like a waterfall.

I had gone back and forth on whether or not I should drink. I'd read that the children of alcoholics are four times as likely to develop problems with alcohol, but I figured there wasn't much point in trying to avoid my mother's legacy. Her face bled into my thoughts as the cheap vodka slid down my throat. I hated the taste and I fought to keep

31

from showing it. It was the same liquor my mom would slip into her morning orange juice. The same taste that made her salivate only ever made me want to gag.

I wiped an excess drop from my lip and passed the bottle on to Trent. He took it with a smirk, skimming his finger against mine, and I knew I'd probably end up going home with him.

"Do you have a boyfriend?" he asked brazenly, emboldened by the vodka. I glanced up to meet Ashley's gaze across the gazebo. She smiled and gave me a subtle thumbs-up. She was impressed I'd caught Trent's attention, but I didn't deserve her praise. I was just the newest and shiniest thing at the party, a glorified spoon for Trent to catch his own reflection in.

I turned to him and slid an inch closer. "No. Why do you care?"

He smiled and focused on my lips as he pulled a little plastic bag out of the pocket of his jeans. Ten little white pills. Molly. I'd never met her, but I'd tried her friends, always hoping that one of them would answer my question: which little white pill makes mothers forget their daughters?

I opened my mouth and Trent slid the pill onto my tongue. The capsule started to dissolve just as he leaned in and kissed me. I pressed my hands against his chest and pushed against him, but he broke the kiss off first. It was quick, painless, innocent, and then the vodka slipped back around to me.

It was time for another sip.

CHAPTER EIGHT

Chase

I **STARED AT** the Calloways' dining table as my lasagna warmed in the microwave. It was an old wooden square that rocked back and forth on unstable legs. It'd sat in the corner of their kitchen for the last decade and a half and it housed countless memories. I'd sat across from Lilah at that table, licking ice cream off my face before begging her to let me finish off her bowl too. I'd lost my first tooth in an apple at that table and I'd gotten in big trouble when I'd scared Lilah with my bloody mouth.

There was a layer of dust coating the top of it now, as if no one had eaten on it in years. I wet a rag and wiped it down until the microwave dinged. Then I took a seat at my old spot against the wall and ate my dinner. I had a perfect view of the empty house. It had the effect of a museum preserving time as best as it could. I knew the lamp in the corner no longer worked, but no one replaced it, just like the ancient VCR and the broken rocking chair in the corner. They were all things Mrs. Calloway had added to the house and I couldn't figure out why no one had gotten rid of them.

I could hear the faint sound of game footage coming from Coach's room down the hall. His notepads littered the house, continuous ramblings of a man with a passion for baseball. I loved the game too, but it was in Mr. Calloway's blood in a way it would never be in mine.

Harvey let out a melodramatic moan beneath the table and I realized he'd been waiting patiently for a scrap. I tossed him a piece of burnt cheese just before the front door opened.

It was 12:01 AM, officially the start of my second day living with the Calloways, and I was finally getting my first glimpse of Lilah. She stumbled inside, closed the door behind her, and then leaned against it as if she couldn't hold up the weight of her own body. With bated breath, I waited for her next move. Before she could meet my gaze, Harvey's excitement bubbled over. I reached down and held his collar so he couldn't run and lunge at her. I shook my head as his bright pleading eyes met mine.

He wanted to run and greet her as much as I did. Lilah was back. She was back, and yet she was so different. Black hair and short shorts and a drug-induced haze. But she was also the same girl I'd always known—pale, small, freckled, and lost. I scraped my chair back and stood to announce my presence, but she was already gone. Her eyes popped open and she ran for the stairs, clutching her stomach with one hand and covering her mouth with the other. She was too sick to notice me standing in the kitchen.

I put Harvey outside and then took the stairs two at a time. We were sharing a bathroom, her and I. She would have noticed my shaving cream beside hers, but her head was over the toilet and she was throwing up, making deep loud heaves that sounded as if her body was rejecting everything inside of her.

I stepped into the bathroom and closed the door carefully so her dad wouldn't hear over the game footage. She reached for toilet paper, wiped her mouth, and whirled around to stare at me.

Her eyes hit me all at once, bright green and vulnerable until she registered who I was.

"Are you okay?" I asked, taking another tentative step closer.

She narrowed her eyes and pointed at the door. "GET OUT."

"Lilah—"

She spun back around and threw up again, her protests about my presence losing to her body's need to purge itself of the night's indiscretions.

"Did you drink?" I asked.

She nodded, quick and almost imperceptible.

"Did you take something too?"

She didn't respond, so I repeated the question. "Lilah, did you take anything?"

"Molly," she said, resting her head on her arm along the edge of the toilet.

I reached around her to flush and caught a whiff of her. She smelled like she'd bathed in cigarette smoke and throw up. I bent low to check if she was all right. Her eyes were closed, her lips cracked and raw. I watched her chest, trying to make out the rise and fall beneath her tank top.

I could feel the heat rolling off of her and after I confirmed she was still breathing, I crept back down the stairs for a glass of water, and then thought better of it and got two.

When I returned, she was awake and sitting with her back against the bathtub. Her knees were pulled to her chest and her hands were wrapped around them, keeping her body in a tight ball.

"Here, drink these," I said, dropping the glasses near her feet and looking away before she could shoot me another death stare.

I rifled through the medicine cabinet above the toilet. Everything in it was old or empty. The only bottle of Advil had expired the year before but I still grabbed it. She'd need something to curb the headache in the morning.

"The prodigal daughter returns," she slurred with a dark tone. "And who runs to meet her?"

I turned from the medicine cabinet to catch her staring up at me with the same fury as before.

"None other than Chase Matthews, *the golden boy himself*." She smirked and wiped the back of her hand across her mouth. "Is this how you expected to find me? Just like *her?*"

CHAPTER NINE

November 1996
Blackwater, Texas

THE OLD HOUSE sat silent in the night except for the two teenage girls trying in vain to keep quiet in the bathroom. Hannah propped Elaine up over the toilet and held her long blonde hair away from her face.

"Shhhh. My parents are going to be back any second and I don't want them to hear us," Hannah warned. "They'll know we're drunk."

Elaine giggled. "I'm not drunk. Are you drunk?"

Hannah rolled her eyes and leaned forward to ensure Elaine's head was positioned over the toilet. They'd already made a mess in her room, something she'd have to deal with as soon as she got Elaine to sleep.

"Chris was so cute tonight. Did you see him?"

"Elaine. I was with you when you were talking to him."

Elaine erupted into another fit of giggles that eventually gave way to dry heaves. Hannah rubbed her friend's back, trying to contain her own urge to throw up. They'd both had too many beers, but there had been a real cause to celebrate. Hannah had received a letter from the University of Texas in the mail earlier that morning. She'd been granted early acceptance into their nursing program. It was her first choice school and her first choice city. She was thrilled, her parents were thrilled, and most importantly, Elaine was thrilled.

As soon as they graduated, they'd leave Blackwater together and never look back.

CHAPTER TEN

Lilah

MY MOTHER'S EYES were a shade of pale green that as a child I swore looked like gemstones. I'd sit with her out in the garden when I was little and the sun would shine so bright I'd have to squint to see her face, but those green eyes could always find me through the glare.

I was dreaming of her green eyes—the same green eyes that stared back at me every time I looked in the mirror—when something cold and wet pressed against my cheek. I jolted out of my dream only to feel the strange sensation again. I blinked my eyes open just in time to see a fat pink tongue reach out and lick from my chin up to my mouth.

"What the hell?!" I screamed and bolted up in my bed.

"Harvey! Get out of there. Harvey! C'mon!"

I had one fraction of a second when all the pieces of the puzzle fell into place before I realized Chase was standing

in my doorway. Shirtless.

"Bad dog," Chase frowned, eyeing his dog like he was about to throw him out the window.

He was toeing the invisible line of my bedroom, trying to retrieve Harvey without encroaching on my territory. I reached for my comforter and tried to conceal my white tank top.

His short blond hair was still mussed from sleep, but every other piece of his appearance was in place: straight nose, strong jaw, golden tan, and lips that I knew could stretch into a grin that would make my toes curl. He wasn't wearing a shirt and his pajama pants sat low on his hips. I took in the slope of his stomach as he bent down to lure Harvey back to him.

"He didn't get to meet you last night," Chase said, giving up and standing to cross his arms over his chest.

Last night.

Last night.

My cheeks burned with a blush I knew Chase could see.

I pulled my gaze away from him and looked back down at Harvey. He was wagging his tail and eyeing me with so much love that it was impossible not to reach over and pat his head. His blond fur was silky soft and the moment my hand connected with him, he stepped closer and rested his chin on the top of my comforter.

I had always wanted a dog.

"He can stay," I said, keeping my eyes on Harvey.

"Are you sure?" Chase asked.

I nodded without looking back up. The image of Chase was already burned into my memory; there was no need to make it worse.

I heard a chuckle and then a moment later the door shut and I was alone again—well, alone with Harvey.

I patted the top of my bed. "C'mon."

Not two seconds later, that massive dog was twirling in a circle on top of my blanket, making himself at home. He tucked into a ball by my side and rested his head on my chest. I stared down into his eyes, reminded of my earlier dream. In the light of day, bright brown eyes were much more comforting than pale green.

CHAPTER ELEVEN

Chase

I STOOD OUTSIDE Lilah's bedroom wondering where Harvey's loyalty would lie at the end of the day. I hadn't seen Lilah like that in years; she'd presented a very different version of herself the night before with dark clothes, dark hair, and an expression that did a fairly good job of warning me away. Just then, however, I'd seen a glimpse of the Lilah I had known before, soft eyes, freckles and all. I'd wanted to follow Harvey into her bedroom and lock us away the rest of the day.

Instead, I turned back for my new room across the hall. I was still getting used to the size. It was small, more like a storage space than an actual bedroom. The old queen bed took up most of the room and the boxes in the corner made it hard to use what little space was leftover.

I made it a point to ignore the boxes. Every time I

glanced over them my chest tightened in anger. Even after a year and a half, I hated the woman down to the very marrow of her bones, bones that now lay in the earth—where they belonged.

My phone buzzed on the bed and I reached over to see the text messages that had started to accumulate.

Brian: Basketball at the school courts at 2? Connor's in.

Connor: Let's party at Kimberly's after basketball. Aren't her parents out of town?

Kimberly: Hey C. My parents are still MIA. Let's celebrate the last day of winter break tonight at my house! Let me know. XO

I didn't bother responding to any of them. Those people—my high school friends—didn't seem to belong in the Calloways' house. They weren't part of my history, not like Lilah was. I needed five more minutes where I could recreate the image of her on her bed. Five more minutes to linger in the past.

CHAPTER TWELVE

Lilah

MONDAY MORNING ARRIVED with a crash of banging pots and another round of dog licks courtesy of Harvey. He hadn't left my side the day before, partly because I'd remained in bed the entire day, reading and napping, and partly because I'd let him have half of my dinner. Either way, I wasn't surprised to find him in my bed on Monday morning, hovering over me with wide eyes and an eternally wagging tail.

I groaned as I rolled out from under my covers and slid into a standard pair of loose jeans, Converse, and a long-sleeved black shirt. While I swiped on my eyeliner and mascara, I gave myself an internal pep talk. I had one semester of high school left. One semester of dealing with people I wanted to escape, one semester of pretending I belonged in a town that held nothing but sad memories.

Before I'd left for Austin, I'd been on the dance team and had hung out with Chase and the other popular kids. In those days, Chase had been the only person who really knew the unfiltered version of my life. Now, everyone knew my family's crazy. No point trying to hide it any more.

My dad had tried to get me to go to therapy after my mom's death, but the ones in Austin were too expensive. I knew how much stress he was already under, so I told him and my aunt I didn't need it. I told them therapy wouldn't bring her back and "besides, I'm fine." I believed I'd figure out how to move on and I promised to tell him if it ever got to the point where I needed help.

We hadn't talked about it since and I wasn't sure whose fault that was.

• • •

When I walked downstairs after getting ready for school, I located the source of the banging pots that had originally jarred me awake. Chase was scrambling eggs and flipping pancakes, all while Harvey sat at his feet, hoping to get a sample of his creations.

I whistled for Harvey and he trotted over, drawing Chase's attention as well.

"Hungry?" he asked.

I breathed in the sight of him. It was something I'd never get used to: that easy smile and his familiar hazel eyes. At least this time he was wearing a shirt.

The smell of maple syrup almost convinced me to give in, but I shook my head.

"I'm fine," I said, moving to the fridge and reaching inside for a carton of orange juice. I poured myself a glass and took small sips as I tried to comprehend the extreme awkwardness of the situation. Chase was cooking breakfast in my kitchen. He was scrambling eggs and flipping pancakes like it was the most normal thing in the world.

"Lilah! Need a ride to school?" my dad asked, running out of his room in khakis and a white polo with "Blackwater Baseball" embroidered over the breast pocket. He was clearly in a rush.

"Nah, go ahead."

He grabbed his baseball cap and tugged it on, already halfway out the door. "Okay. Be home for dinner later. I'll whip up something to celebrate your first day back!"

The front door slammed shut behind him, shaking the front windows and highlighting the fact that Chase and I were now very alone in my house.

Out of the corner of my eye, I watched Chase turn off the stove, shovel eggs and pancakes onto two plates, and set them down on the kitchen table across from one another.

He chose the side facing me, sat down, and cut off my line of sight to the windows so that I had no choice but to meet his eyes or cave and look away.

"I made enough for the both of us," he said as he doused his pancakes with what looked like two gallons of syrup.

"I don't normally eat breakfast."

He arched a brow, scooped up a big bite of eggs, and then smiled at me while he chewed. I could not wrap my head around him. Didn't he understand how this situation was supposed to play out? We were meant to ignore each other's existence and go about business as usual.

We sat in uncomfortable silence as I sipped my juice and he finished off his breakfast. As I moved to wash out my cup, he hopped out of his seat and came to stand directly behind me so he could reach around and place his dish in the sink. His arm skimmed my waist and I tried to stay calm as his height eclipsed mine.

"I think we should ride to school together," he said, finally taking a step back.

I released a breath I hadn't realized I was holding.

"No thanks," I answered simply.

He crossed his arms. "Lilah, it makes sense. We're both going to the same place."

"I like to walk."

"That was before you moved away. Now, I can give you a ride."

He smiled and my thoughts slid away. The full extent of his smile was something that could only be processed in pieces. Matching dimples, straight teeth—it was the source of all of his power.

I shook away my momentary paralysis.

"I like walking. It clears my head," I said, moving to put distance between us and retrieve my backpack from the kitchen doorway.

Just as I slung the strap over my shoulder, I heard metal clang against the kitchen table. When I turned, I saw his car keys sitting on top of the worn wood, directly over the spot where my mom had always sat.

"All right, then I'll walk with you," he declared.

CHAPTER THIRTEEN

Chase

I HAD KNOWN Lilah would be a challenge, but she was proving to be more complex than any of my old cameras. No one in their right mind turned down my pancakes. They were the best in Blackwater—probably the world—fluffy and soft, yet crisp and golden brown. I sat at the table, watching her take sips of orange juice, and tried to pretend that the fluffy dough and maple syrup were enough to occupy my mind. In reality, I was thinking of how to break the ice between us. I wanted to just shout, "It's not your fault. It's not my fault. Let's forgive each other and move on." But, something told me Lilah wouldn't respond to a direct apology like that. She was a feral cat. I had to coax her into trusting me slowly, and walking to school with her was just the beginning.

Blackwater High School was only about a mile away

from Lilah's house, and I had no problem leaving my truck behind in favor of walking alongside her. The second we bid farewell to Harvey—who was not pleased to be left behind—she pulled out her iPod and cut herself off from the rest of world.

The message was clear, but I ignored it.

"So you like orange juice for breakfast, huh? Vitamin C, right?"

No answer.

I could hear her music blaring through her headphones and I knew she couldn't hear a single world I was saying.

"I like it too. It's good when you make it with fresh squeezed oranges. Remember when we kept burying whole oranges in your backyard to try to get trees to grow? Didn't we go a year before your dad told us they were seedless?"

No answer, but I swore she picked up her pace. It wasn't a challenge to keep up—I was nearly a foot taller than her and she was already taking two steps to each one of mine—but the idea that she was trying to get away from me made me laugh.

"Yeah, good times," I answered wistfully.

Usually before school, I pulled my truck into my designated spot in the student parking lot and hung around outside with my friends until classes started. Lilah had usually joined me before she moved away, but something told me the student lot was no longer her scene.

As we rounded the sidewalk to the front of the school, our separate worlds unfolded before us. I could already see Connor, Brian, and Kimberly hanging around my spot. A few guys from the baseball team waved to me from behind the chain-link fence near the front of the lot and I nodded back.

Lilah slowed down and pulled back from me until I had

to either stop walking or leave her behind.

I glanced back to find her attention focused ahead of us and when I followed her line of sight, I came face to face with Trent Bailey.

He'd been leaning against the giant oak tree that sat in the direct center of the front lawn. The stoners had claimed it as their territory since the dawn of time. The second he'd spotted Lilah, he pushed off the tree and walked to meet her.

I fought against my better judgment to try and stop her from heading over to him. *Since when does she hang out with Trent Bailey?*

My fists clenched by my sides.

"Lilah—" I said, not sure of where my sentence would lead.

She brushed by me and walked toward Trent like she was greeting an old friend. Suddenly, I was the outsider, the voyeur. Still, I couldn't make myself move. I stood paralyzed and confused, staring at her dark hair as if I'd find answers hidden in the dark strands.

He reached out for her hand and I flinched back to reality. I wouldn't watch her go down that path. I turned to walk away just as she turned back to find me over her shoulder. It was a gift she was offering. Not quite a smile, not really. It was only the tip of her mouth, the right corner lifting in solidarity.

It was hardly anything at all. An untrained eye would have missed it altogether, but I knew what she was doing. I'd seen that look every time I'd pissed Lilah off when we were growing up. It was her tell, the first sign that she was starting to come around and forgive me.

Come back to me, Lilah.

CHAPTER FOURTEEN

Lilah

"WHY WERE YOU just walking with Chase Matthews?" Trent asked as we walked to join the group of kids hanging out under the oak tree at the front of the high school. I tucked my headphones away in my bag, taking a moment to gather my bearings after my walk with Chase.

"Why do you care?" I asked, annoyed with the edge of ownership in Trent's voice. He and I were not a couple. We were hardly friends.

"He's a preppy douche, Lilah," Trent said, trying to wrap his arm around my waist. I took a step away instead.

"Thanks for the tip," I answered haughtily just as Ashley walked up to the group. Her blonde hair was air-dried and wavy, the pink streaks brighter than ever. She'd taken the time to perfect her makeup before school, a concept I couldn't find the will to get behind. Still, she looked pretty.

"Who's got some they wouldn't mind sharing?" she asked with a laugh, tapping her shoulder against mine. "There's no way I'll get through first period straight."

A small kid on the other side of Trent started rolling a joint, trying to hide his actions inside his unzipped backpack. He was doing a half-assed job and anyone with half a brain would have been able to discern what he was doing if they'd happened to walk by. I had five months in this hellhole and nothing was going to jeopardize that.

I stepped away from the group and headed for the front doors of the school, not bothering with goodbyes. The first bell was going to ring in a few minutes anyway and I still had to go to the front office and pick up my class schedule.

Trent called out after me, "Lilah, let's hang out after school!"

I waved to him over my shoulder and kept walking, trying to remember what I'd found appealing about him in the first place.

● ● ●

I should have gone up to the high school early to finalize my class schedule. The front office was packed with kids trying to switch their classes around. They were all sitting there with their yellow schedules on their laps, scribbling out the classes they didn't want to take and trying desperately to replace them with something easier. I wished I could have just grabbed one of their schedules and left. Sitting through advanced auto-mechanics beat listening to a bunch of whiny seniors beg for free periods.

"Ms. Calloway." A short, round secretary tried to find me in the crowd of students. "Ms. Calloway," she called again.

I pushed to my feet and made my way toward the door behind the reception desk. I'd been to the counselor's office a few times before I'd moved, and the shock of familiarity made me pause in the doorway. The scent of cheap cologne, a half-dead ivy sitting in the corner, a tall, bald man sitting behind his desk, desperately guzzling down his coffee between student appointments. His name was Mr. Joy, which was ironic considering he'd been the one to deliver the news of my mother's death.

He glanced up from his coffee to find me standing in the doorway and beckoned me closer.

"Lilah, come in. Come in."

I moved to take a seat as he tried to find his keyboard beneath the scattered papers on his desk, all the while gulping down long swallows of coffee.

"First day," he laughed, explaining away the mess.

I sat silent, slipping my hands beneath my legs so I wouldn't be tempted to touch anything on his desk. I bet there were so many secrets waiting to be found: student records and changed schedules, progress reports and letters of expulsion. Who wasn't passing pre-cal? Whose parents were calling the school every day, checking to make sure their kid wasn't cutting class?

"Your high school back in Austin emailed me over your records last week," Mr. Joy confirmed, typing away on his keyboard.

He hit enter and a squeaky printer behind him spat out my new schedule. He handed it over and I scanned down the list of classes. No Advanced Placement Environmental Science, nor AP Spanish or Statistics.

"I was taking all AP classes back in Austin."

He frowned. "I saw that. Unfortunately, we don't offer as many AP classes here, but I'm sure colleges will understand given your…circumstances."

Circumstances was a euphemism for things he didn't have the courage to say.

I glanced up to find him studying me. "You know, Lilah, while I have you here, it might be a good time to schedule a one-on-one counseling session. We could talk about your time spent in Austin and what your plans are for the future."

I folded my schedule in half and stood. "Actually, I better get to my first class."

"Lilah, I know that the last year and a half haven't been easy for you."

I ignored him and pointed to the ivy plant in the corner. "You need to water that. It's almost dead."

Honestly, why would I want counseling from a man who lets his plants die?

Ivy is the easiest thing to take care of. Water it and stick it in a window.

I turned and made my way back through the crowded office, happy to be free of Mr. Joy's kindly stare. I glanced down at my schedule and ticked off the classes I'd like: AP Physics, English Lit, and AP Art History. Then I scanned over the classes that would undoubtedly bore me. I was trading in AP Environmental Science to be a teacher's aide for a freshman English class. What a royal waste of time.

"Lilah! Lilah Calloway? Is that you?"

I glanced up from my schedule to find Kimberly White standing in the hallway a few feet in front of me. She was helping a group of dance team girls unravel a huge banner that said "Welcome Back to School" in bright, scrolling letters. Each one of them was wearing a different version of the same outfit: tight jeans, knee-high boots, and a cashmere sweater. They looked like a Macy's ad. Kimberly abandoned them to greet me and I swallowed down a lump of jealousy.

In another life, I was supposed to be Kimberly. Freshman and sophomore year of high school we'd been co-captains of the high school dance team, blonde, and popular—but I was popular by proxy. Chase had pulled me into the spotlight but Kimberly was destined to be there. She'd been dealt a perfect hand in life, one that included good genes, a sweet disposition, and rich, doting parents. Her dad was the only dentist in Blackwater and when she smiled, I was reminded of the fact that she'd had braces not once, but twice. A perfect smile for a perfect girl.

"I can't believe you're back," she said, beaming at me after she'd engulfed me in a one-sided hug. "You look so cute with that haircut, like Emma Watson or something!"

"Oh, thanks," I said, trying to casually sidestep her. First bell was about to ring and I had no clue where my first class was.

She noticed my retreat with grace. "Oh, duh! You have to get to class. Why don't you come find me during lunch? We can catch up!"

I nodded, although I was confused by what she meant. I didn't need to catch Kimberly up on my life; she and the rest of that small town knew every sordid detail from beginning to end. My family's secrets had been plucked, pressed, preserved, and put on display.

It wasn't fair that everyone knew my secrets but I didn't know theirs. The scales were tipped in their favor, and since I couldn't erase the secrets on my side, it was time to start weighing down theirs.

CHAPTER FIFTEEN

June 1997
Blackwater, Texas

GRADUATION DAY SYMBOLIZED freedom. Elaine and Hannah had counted down the days, marking them off one by one until they could finally don their creased graduation gowns and walk across the stage once and for all. Blackwater High didn't have much of a budget for a graduation ceremony, which meant each year it took place out on the football field, on top of the dry summer grass with the twinkling stadium lights usually reserved for Friday nights in the fall.

Elaine cursed the poor lighting in the stadium bathroom as she tried in vain to flatten her hair beneath her graduation cap. No matter how much she worked with them, the pale blonde strands wouldn't cooperate. If she'd had it her way, she and Hannah would have skipped graduation altogether. There was no point in her being there. Her mom was working a late shift and her dad was rotting away in a jail across the state. No one would be cheering for her in the stands.

"Okay, I give up with my hair. Are you almost done in there?" Elaine asked, spinning around to face the stall Hannah had locked herself inside ten minutes earlier. "We're gonna be late."

When Hannah didn't respond, Elaine stepped closer and pressed her ear to the stall door, trying to hear Hannah over the noise of the stadium.

"Oh my god, c'mon!" someone yelled from the back of the long line. "There are other people waiting!"

The bathroom was small, only three stalls in total, and Hannah had occupied one of them for too long.

"Hannah?" Elaine asked, trying to coax her friend out before mob mentality took over.

When Hannah didn't reply, Elaine crouched down to look beneath the stall door. Hannah was pacing back and forth in the tiny space.

She frowned. "Hannah. What are you doing?" She stood and rattled the locked door. "Let me in."

For the past few weeks Elaine had noticed that Hannah was off. She hadn't wanted to talk about their approaching move to Austin, she hadn't wanted to browse through classified ads for apartments. Elaine had assumed she was getting cold feet, but as Hannah opened the door to let Elaine step into the stall with her, she feared it was much, much worse.

Hannah's graduation cap was upside down on the bathroom floor, dirty and forgotten. Her graduation gown was unzipped and falling off her shoulder. Her makeup was smeared and her tears were carrying mascara down her cheeks in splotchy black lines.

Elaine stepped closer, trying to console her friend, and that's when Hannah unfolded her fists, revealing the slim pregnancy test hidden inside. Two little pink lines stretched across the results window.

Those two pink lines took their best-laid plans and turned them to dust.

"I'm pregnant," she whispered.

CHAPTER SIXTEEN

Chase

HALFWAY THROUGH LILAH'S first day back, I walked into the cafeteria with my tray of food and tried to find her. Even though most everyone had grown up together, the jocks still ate with the jocks and so on. Everyone had their unofficial assigned spot—everyone except for Lilah.

She was nowhere to be found. I took the long way to my seat and then looped around the room once more. Finally, I circled back to the entrance of the cafeteria and slid into the last open seat at my table of friends.

"Took you long enough," Connor laughed.

I brushed off his comment and worked on my hamburger wrapper, barely managing to unwrap it before they jumped in on my living situation. They all knew my dad was a drunk, so they weren't surprised that I'd moved out—they were just surprised by where I'd ended up.

"I can't believe you used to be friends with Lilah

Calloway," Connor blurted out after taking a massive bite of his burger. "She's in my second period and she scares the hell out of me."

Kimberly spoke up before I could. "She's actually really nice. We used to be on dance team together."

Connor had moved to our town at the beginning of junior year, so he'd never known the pre-loner version of Lilah. Even the kids who'd grown up with her hardly remembered that version of her, which is why I was surprised Kimberly was sticking up for her.

"Well, I think she's hotter now than she was before. She looks like a sexy vampire or something," Brian added.

I threw my burger wrapper at his head.

"You're full of shit."

"I said a SEXY vampire!" he clarified, holding his hands up in surrender and looking to Connor for backup. None came.

I narrowed my eyes at him, wondering how many other guys at school had a thing for Lilah. Trent sure as hell did.

"Kim, do you know if Lilah and Trent are dating?" I asked, picking up a handful of fries.

Connor perked up like a dog begging for a bone. "Does the almighty Chase Matthews want to be an Edward to her Bella?"

I ignored him and glanced toward Kimberly.

She was fidgeting with something in her purse. "Oh, I'm not sure. Didn't she just move back to town?"

"Yeah, on Saturday."

She zipped up her purse with a forceful tug. "I can ask around if you want?"

I shrugged, trying to think of a good excuse for why I'd care about Lilah's love life. "Yeah, I just hate that kid, so if he's going to be hanging around her house, I'd like to know."

She nodded, still not meeting my eyes, and I wondered if I'd made a mistake. Kimberly and I had dated off and on the year before, but we'd been friends—just friends—for a while. Asking her for help with Lilah probably wasn't the smartest move, but I needed to know.

• • •

AP Physics was my last class before baseball practice and the teacher, Mr. Jenkins, had a way of making the forty-five minute period stretch on for what felt like hours. I walked into the classroom and arced my empty water bottle into the recycling bin near his desk. It landed smoothly inside the bin, but Mr. Jenkins still glared at me over the top of his 80s-style reading glasses and pointed his finger at my desk.

"Find your seat, Mr. Matthews."

Apparently he hadn't found a personality over winter break, which meant the last semester of his class would be just as unbearable as the first.

I turned to join Connor at our table and then froze when I saw Lilah standing in the back of the room with her arms crossed and her eyes pinned on me. I hadn't seen her all day, not in the morning assembly or in the hallways between classes. I smiled. She'd avoided me all day, but apparently she and I would be in the same sixth period for the next few months.

Our physics class was set up so that everyone worked in pairs. Each pair shared a small black table, which explained why Lilah was standing by herself: she didn't have an assigned seat yet. I dropped my backpack on my chair and then glanced around the room. Mr. Jenkins had paired us up the semester before, so unless someone had dropped the course, Lilah would have to work alone or join a team of two.

"*Edward*, stop staring and sit," Connor said.

I ignored him and headed back toward Mr. Jenkins' desk. He pretended not to notice me at first, but I cleared my throat, and finally his gray hair tilted back and his annoyed stare met mine.

"How was your winter break, Mr. Jenkins?" I asked with a smile.

He narrowed his eyes. "Go back to your seat, Mr. Matthews."

"Actually, I wanted to ask you if Lilah Calloway could join Connor and me at our table? Since there's an odd number and all."

Connor groaned and a few students laughed. I kept my focus on Mr. Jenkins as he leaned to the side to look at Lilah standing in the back of the class. It looked like he'd only just realized she was back there. He studied her and then glanced back at me, trying to work out my angle.

I widened my smile and shrugged.

"Lilah, pull a chair up to their table," he said, returning his attention to the work on his desk. "You'll work with Chase and Connor this semester."

"Uh, actually, I can just work alone," she protested with a calm, firm voice.

Mr. Jenkins sighed and shook his head. "No. We work in pairs in this class, or in your case, a trio."

"But I was in AP Physics at my old school. I'm sure I can manage on my own."

He closed his eyes, pulled the glasses from his face, and massaged the skin beside the bridge of his nose. "Please, just do as I ask."

The subject was closed.

I smiled and turned to face Lilah. Her bright eyes were furious. Every student in the class had turned to watch her and a deep blush spread across her cheeks and neck. I pulled a chair from the corner of the room, shoved Connor toward the window, and dropped the empty chair on the other side of mine.

She waited until the final bell rang and then she took the seat beside me, positioning herself on the chair so that she was as far away from me as possible.

"Is this your idea of a joke?" she whispered as Mr. Jenkins stood to begin that day's lesson.

I pulled out my notebook and shook my head.

"No joke. My plan is to win you back one physics problem at a time."

Connor laughed. "Does this make me Jacob?"

Lilah ignored the both of us as Mr. Jenkins started drawing out an equation on the blackboard. For the first time I could remember, I was excited to be in Mr. Jenkins' physics class.

CHAPTER SEVENTEEN

Lilah

I KNEW FROM years past that Chase had baseball practice after school Monday through Thursday, so I didn't bother waiting for him after the final bell rang. I put my headphones in, pressed play on my iPod, and broke through the crowded hallway until I reached the side door of the school. I pushed it open and inhaled a deep breath of fresh air.

On days like that, when winter was retreating and I could finally feel the sun again, it was hard to remember why I hated springtime so much. That crisp air should have held possibilities, but I'd take one step into spring and the sad memories would fling back into my thoughts so hard I'd have to pinch my eyelids closed to control the residual pain.

My mother had been a chameleon and for seven years

she'd worn one appearance: mother. She had fit the role so well it was hard for me to wrap my head around her being anything but perfect. Before I was seven, my memories of her were all good and happy—what they should have been. Maybe that's why it had blindsided me so much when one day she'd packed her bags and explained that she couldn't live with us any more. She didn't want to be married, she didn't want to be a mother—she wanted her freedom.

It was springtime when my mother had left us for the first time. I was seven. It was hard to know what was going on then—when my mother walked out that day, my dad gave me a G-rated version of the truth—but now that I'd had eleven years to study the memories and form them into coherent events, it all made sense.

Freedom.

At the time, I was confused about why she couldn't have freedom with us, and then I realized that freedom was a euphemism, and a poor one at that. To her, freedom represented everything she had been forced to give up because of me—partying, and pills, and strange men.

I'd tried hard to get her to stay that day.

I ran out of the house after her, but my dad held me back. I screamed for her out on our porch stairs as she lugged two broken suitcases toward the old black Camaro waiting for her at the end of our driveway. The car rumbled so loudly that at first, I thought she couldn't hear me crying. I screamed louder as she loaded the suitcases in the backseat and the guy sitting behind the wheel turned to stare at me. He dangled a cigarette between his fingers and I could see the dark tattoos snaked around his arm. He had a black baseball hat pulled low, covering his eyes, and after my mom slid into the passenger seat beside him, he drove that car away as fast as possible, squealing his tires on the pavement.

My mother had never turned back.

The memory of that day faded as I rounded the corner to see my house sitting empty and quiet. Nothing had changed. I could still picture the black Camaro in the driveway even though the tire marks had faded years ago.

I walked up the front path, ready to ascend the rickety stairs, when suddenly, I hesitated. There was nothing for me inside that house. My dad and Chase were both at baseball practice. I had no homework and no new secrets to revel in. I had nothing to distract myself from old memories. I reached for my phone and texted Trent out of impulse.

Lilah: Are you home?

After I hit send, I turned and sat down at the foot of the porch stairs, trying to get the image of my mother out of my mind. A second later, my phone buzzed.

Trent: About to be. Come over, my mom is working a double.

I knew I was running from my past as I pushed off the porch and started to head in the direction of Trent's house. I knew it, and yet I didn't care. I wanted a temporary salve and that's what he would be.

It was a short walk to the poor neighborhood across Main Street. Trent was waiting for me when I reached his old bungalow house. He kicked the screen door open and shot me a knowing glance as I walked up the gravel path. A stray tabby cat crossed in front of me, starring up at me with nervous eyes.

"Just couldn't stay away?" he asked with a charming smirk. I wanted to tell him how little he meant to me—to wipe that smirk right off his face—but I shrugged and moved past him through the doorway. The scent of mildew hit me right away.

"Want to smoke?" he asked, already heading to find his stash.

"I'm fine. Let's just go to your room. I have to be back before my dad gets home from practice. He wants to eat dinner as a family."

My dad wouldn't care if I was late, but the excuse would justify my quick departure.

I dropped my backpack in the front entry and followed him to his room, trying to ignore the sadness that emanated from his quiet house. I knew Trent's world was marred with memories just as terrible as mine. He never talked about his dad, but everyone gossips in a small town, and no one can resist the juicy details of a parent's early departure. I knew that better than anyone.

We moved through his dark house until we reached his room. The stench of ancient smoke was impossible to miss. There were yellow stains across the carpet of indiscernible origins and posters covering every available surface of his walls. When I reached his bed, I kicked off my shoes and fell back onto the worn sheets. Trent followed me into his room and sat at his desk to light up.

If I held my breath, I could pretend his sheets smelled like the shower gel that had appeared in our upstairs bathroom upon Chase's arrival. I'd used it that morning on a whim, wanting to see if his scent could rub off on me.

It wasn't the sex that kept me going back to guys like Trent; that part wasn't even that great. It was afterward, when we lay in bed. For a few minutes I pretended that I was a girl that was loved and could love. I pretended that instead of another sad kid—a nameless guy—they were my soulmate, a boy I'd known my whole life.

I tried to push the sadness away. I didn't know why it was hitting me there of all places. I was supposed to be there to run from my memories, but even when I closed my eyes and fisted Trent's sheets between my fingers, I had the sudden urge to scream.

Shit.

I had to get out.

I pushed off his bed and went to grab my shoes.

"Where are you going?" he asked, spinning in his desk chair, not bothering to pause rolling his joint.

"Sorry, I totally spaced. My dad is getting home early today. I'll see you at school," I stammered before leaving his room. I retrieved my backpack from the entry, forced my Converse on, and pushed through the screen door.

The smell of spring hit me again and I squeezed my eyes closed. In late January, the air was crisp and clean. None of the humid heat that swept in during the summer had made an appearance yet. I longed for that humidity. I longed for the stifling heat. It meant I had three whole seasons to prepare myself before spring came again.

• • •

When I got home, I leaned back on the dead grass in my backyard, crossed my legs, and stared out at the remnants of the garden positioned behind our small cottage house. My dad had already fixed up the flowerbeds. The wood was mismatched, new and old, fresh and worn. There were eight beds in total and if I planned them out right, I could fill every last inch of them with seeds.

I scribbled down combinations in my journal, each one specifically chosen for companion growing. Tansy and roses grow well together because tansy attracts ladybugs and ladybugs eat aphids before they can harm the roses. Onions grown near carrots usually keep away the rust flies and broccoli paired with cucumbers helps to repel beetles. There were more combinations, hundreds and hundreds, but my mom had only taught me a few before she'd left.

Harvey lay sprawled in the grass beside me, content to bask in the late evening sun as I patted his belly. I was still trying to recall more planting combinations when a shadow fell over my notebook. I glanced up to find Chase standing there, his blond hair damp with sweat. Unless I could find planting techniques tattooed across his arms, there was no reason to keep staring at him, but I hadn't seen his body up close in years. He hardly looked like the boy I'd grown up with. That kid had been scrawny and tall. The Chase standing beside me was suddenly a man.

"What are you two doing?" he asked, jarring me out of my intense staring contest with his biceps. When I scanned up to his face, he was wearing a playful smile and the glint in his hazel eyes told me he knew exactly what I'd been doing.

"Planning out my beds," I answered simply before staring back down at my notebook.

He bent to greet Harvey and the dog went crazy, licking and wagging his tail now that his best friend was home.

"I'm pretty good with a shovel if you need any help."

I bit down on my lip, wondering if I'd have to take him up on his offer.

"Harvey's pretty good at digging holes too," he added.

I laughed and the sound surprised me. For a moment, I forgot the balance of the universe, but it didn't last. Chase and I were no longer friends and it had to stay that way.

I pushed off the ground and closed my notebook with a slap.

"I'm going to go start dinner," I said before walking away.

I wanted everything to be simple, but every time I gave Chase a little bit more, a laugh or a smile, I felt guilt wrap around my neck like a vine, choking me inch by inch.

I texted Trent when I got to the kitchen.

Lilah: Sorry I left early today.
Trent: No problem. Are you going to Sasha's party this weekend?
Lilah: I hadn't heard anything about it...
Trent: Well now you have. I'll pick you and Ashley up on my way there.

Balance restored.

CHAPTER EIGHTEEN

June 1997
Deer Valley, Texas

THE FIRST SIX months of Hannah's pregnancy had been a lonely endeavor. There was only one OB/GYN in Blackwater and he had a heart for gossip, so Hannah had researched and found a doctor two towns away in Deer Valley. Her best friend always accompanied her to and from the doctor's office, and it was on the return journey of her six-month checkup that Elaine had announced her news.

"I think I'm pregnant."

Hannah's jaw dropped. "What!? Seriously? With Chris?"

Elaine rolled her eyes. "Of course with Chris. Who else would—"

Hannah cut her off. "Have you done a test yet?"

Elaine glanced out the window and shook her head. "No."

Hannah didn't hesitate before booking Elaine an appointment at the OB/GYN in Deer Valley. They sat together in a dark exam room, the only light coming from the thin window on the door and the ancient ultrasound machine whirring beside the exam chair. Hannah stood to the side, clutching her friend's hand. Elaine stared up at the ceiling, only catching bits and pieces of the appointment: the cold petroleum jelly slipping down her thigh, the scratchy paper covering the exam chair, the doctor's quiet cadence as he explained that she was listening to her baby's heartbeat for the first time.

"Elaine, did you hear the doctor? That's the sound of her heart."

"*Her?*" the doctor questioned, eyeing Hannah with an incredulous glare.

Hannah smiled and reached for her growing belly out of instinct. "Oh, it's just that I'm having a baby boy, so we think—"

The doctor hit print on the ultrasound machine, interrupting her explanation. "She won't know the gender for a few weeks."

Hannah backpedaled. "Yes. Of course."

The doctor flicked on the light in the exam room and Elaine blinked, trying to force her eyes to adjust to the brightness. He held out a photo for her to take and she realized she was seeing her baby for the first time—well, what she assumed was a baby. It could have been anything to her untrained eye. The doctor gave her orders to get dressed and meet him in his office, but Elaine sat immobile, mesmerized by the residual echoes of her baby's heartbeat paired with the image in front of her. The fact that she was pregnant finally sank in; she was going to be a mom. She pressed her hand over her stomach and tried to keep from crying.

"I can't believe we're both going to be moms!" Hannah was elated with the news, bouncing around the room on a cloud that Elaine couldn't see. It made perfect sense to her. They were soulmates, friends, sisters. They were supposed to walk through life arm in arm and that included experiencing motherhood together. "We're young, but that's okay. Our kids will grow up together and they'll even be in the same grade. I think they'll be—"

"Hannah," Elaine cut in. "Do you think some women aren't meant to be mothers?"

Hannah turned and shot her friend a skeptical glare. "What do you mean?"

Elaine furrowed her brows, choosing to stare at a spot on the ceiling rather than meeting her friend's eyes. "Do you think someone with my past should really be responsible for a little life? I have no clue what I'm doing and my family wasn't the best example to learn from."

Hannah tossed Elaine's clothes onto the exam table and threw her hands up in the air. "I don't know what I'm doing either! I'm six months pregnant and I'm just as confused as you are." She crossed the room and reached down to grip her friend's hand. "We can do this together. We'll have each other for support."

Elaine wanted to believe her. Out of the two of them, Hannah was the eternal optimist, a purveyor of hope and possibility. In a perfect world, Hannah and Elaine would both be great mothers and just this once, Elaine wanted to believe in a perfect world.

She'd keep the baby.

CHAPTER NINETEEN

Chase

BY THE TIME I finished hanging out with Brian after the second day back at school, the porch lights were on at the Calloways' house. I let myself in and kicked off my dirty shoes, listening for any sound of life. The TV was on in the living room, but no one was watching it. I'd already eaten dinner at Brian's house, so I bypassed the kitchen and made my way for the stairs, hearing the faint sounds of music as soon as I reached the top.

Lilah was in her room with the door cracked and when I caught sight of her, I stopped dead in my tracks. She was sitting in the center of her queen bed with her homework sprawled out in front of her. Her hair was damp and combed away from her face. She was wearing one of her dad's giant Blackwater Baseball t-shirts, and laying directly beside her—and looking pretty happy about it—was Harvey.

I knocked gently on the door and pushed it open another few inches. She paused flipping through her textbook and glanced up.

"Hi," I offered, lamely.

Connor thought she looked like a sexy vampire, but this was always the best version of Lilah. Just her.

"Hi," she said, eyeing Harvey and then glancing up to me.

The dog didn't even make a move to greet me. He was all too happy to stay right where he was. *Traitor.*

I patted my thigh. "Harvey, c'mon, you need dinner."

He didn't budge.

Lilah put a tentative hand on him. "Oh, um, I didn't know when you'd be home so I fed him. It was the same amount I saw you feed him this morning."

I relaxed back against the doorframe.

"Sorry if that was wrong. I just didn't want him to be hungry," she continued.

Four sentences. Practically a paragraph of text. She hadn't said that much to me since she'd moved away. She could feed my dog every day if it meant she'd start to let me in again.

"Thanks," I said, offering her a smile so she'd know that I meant it.

Her brown eyes held my stare for another moment before she tapped her pencil's eraser on the page of her book.

"I better get back to work," she said.

"Need help?" I asked, eyeing the calculus set she was working through.

"Oh." She paused, as if confused by my question, and then her eyes met mine. "No, actually, I'm working ahead."

I smiled. Of course she was working ahead. She wanted

out of this town as soon as possible.

I tapped my hand on the door, then headed to my room to work on the cameras. The box was beneath my bed was practically overflowing with them. I'd had plans to repair a bunch of them over winter break, but the move had gotten in the way.

I rifled through them, trying my best to create an organized system of triage. A few of them only needed minor work: replacement lenses or rangefinder adjustments. I unwrapped those cameras and lined them up on the small desk in the corner of the room.

Mrs. Calloway's boxes were still stacked beside the desk, but I ignored them and pulled my toolbox from beneath the bed as well. It wasn't the ideal storage space, but the room was too small to store them anywhere else. I'd learned that the first night when I'd left them at the foot of my bed and stubbed my toe on the heavy metal toolbox in the middle of the night.

Once my tools were organized in neat rows, I took a seat and started working. I'd tried to get Connor and Brian into repairing cameras with me. The payout had them interested, but neither one of them loved it the way I did. I think it was the randomness of it that got to them. Each camera was different and there was no simple formula to follow.

I finished up cleaning out an old Canon and then picked up my phone to call my dad. It wasn't one of the numbers called often, so I scrolled through the contacts and hovered over the Ds. He hadn't been home when I'd packed up my truck and left the house on Saturday. I'd figured he would have called by now, seeing as I hadn't been home for the last four days, but there'd been nothing but radio silence.

I hit call, held my phone between my shoulder and ear,

and kept working on the Canon. It rang a dozen or so times and then a generic voicemail kicked on. I hung up and tried the repair shop. No one answered there either, and when the answering machine picked up, it was too full to accept any new messages.

I threw my phone on my bed behind me and went back to work on the Canon. Five minutes later, it was too broken to fix. I'd lost control of the screwdriver and shattered the lens. I ripped out the wires and tore open the heart of the thing, stabbing away at it until it was nearly unrecognizable.

CHAPTER TWENTY

Lilah

FOR THE FIRST two days back at school, Chase had insisted on walking alongside me to school. I could speed up, slow down, turn left when I should have turned right, yet there he'd be. He talked the whole time, even as I blared my music, and I couldn't stand another day of it. I set my alarm for 4 AM on Wednesday morning and shoved my phone beneath my pillow so Chase wouldn't hear the blaring music jar me awake. The last thing I needed was *more* time with him before school.

I had three hours until first bell, and the coffee shop in the town square didn't open until 7 AM. I wiped sleep from my eyes and circled around the town square, trying to find a distraction. The square mimicked the template found in most small Texas towns: shops and restaurants rimmed the perimeter, and smack dab in the middle on a half-acre of green grass stood a town hall made of interlocking limestone blocks. Years ago, the statuesque building had housed city government, but not any more. It cost too much to maintain, so the town had began leasing the first and second floors to a law office and a real estate holding company. The businesses jumped at the prime office space, and Blackwater didn't have to board up its town hall.

The streetlights loomed overhead, drawing every flying insect within a 100-mile radius. I meandered around the square, enjoying the peace and quiet. I loved walking around my small town in the early morning hours; it meant that I could wander free from pitying gazes and conspicuous whispers. Everyone in town knew my past and everyone was eager to see me return—not so they could welcome me back with open arms, but because they needed someone to pity, someone who had a worse life than they did. A busted radiator seemed manageable when compared to a dead mother.

I walked past windows with well-dressed mannequins and a new candle shop that had opened while I'd been away in Austin. My aimless journey eventually ended outside the Matthews' repair shop. The old red sign in the window read 'Closed' and it was tilted off balance, as if someone had been in a hurry to turn it and leave. Out front, piled on the sidewalk against the front door, there were a half dozen boxes and packages left unclaimed.

Dust and dirt had accumulated across the tops of the mailing labels, so I wiped some of it away to confirm that they were all addressed to Mr. Matthews. They'd clearly been sitting out for a few days, but no one had bothered to steal them, which didn't speak highly of the crime rate in our small town; rather, it spoke poorly of the amount of foot traffic the town square usually produced on any given day. Most of the shops didn't stay open longer than a few months; the Matthews' repair shop was a rare exception.

I glanced around to confirm that the square was still deserted and then turned to check the lock on the door. Mr. Matthews used a simple cable lock and when I shined my cell phone's light at the keyhole, I discovered why. There was a key broken off inside that he hadn't bothered to get out. Instead, he'd looped a cable lock between the door handle and a hook on the doorframe. It looked like the work of an overzealous eight-year-old trying to keep his parents out of his room. Anyone with a pair of nail clippers could have torn through the cable.

I tried two combinations on the lock; the first was Hannah's birthday, and the second was Chase's birthday. The lock popped open on the second try and I pulled the door open, covering my ears in anticipation of a blaring alarm. *Of course he doesn't have an alarm, this is Blackwater.* The shop stayed silent as I worked quickly to shove the boxes and packages inside. I was careful not to damage any, but as I stepped back and reviewed my work, I wasn't happy. The boxes were stacked haphazardly on the welcome mat inside the doorway, and more than likely, Mr. Matthews would trip on them when he arrived at work in a few hours. I sighed, checked around me once again, and then walked into the shop.

It felt like stepping into an old memory. The smell hit me right away, that slow decay of old carpet, chipped paint, and air filters in need of replacing. The shop was bare and ugly, but repair shops aren't supposed to be pretty.

I started the arduous task of carrying the heavy boxes from the doorway to the small area behind the counter. I stacked them from heaviest to lightest and pushed them out of the way, into a corner. I thought about leaving a post-it note explaining how I'd broken in and left the boxes, but that would only lead to more questions. He didn't need to know that I was the one to put the boxes inside. If anything, maybe it'd convince him to finally put a proper lock on his front door.

When I was finished, I turned to leave and caught sight of a small photo framed next to the cash register. The colors were faded and a yellow tint had started to creep in near the corners, but I recognized the children in it right away. It was a photo of me and Chase when were little kids. It was a terrible shot, out of focus and shot too close to distinguish anything but our bucktooth grins. Chase had four missing teeth and I had dirt smudged across my cheek. He was squeezing my face to his and I was laughing, my eyes squeezed shut and my smile big and toothy.

I picked up the photo from the counter and stuffed it into my backpack before leaving the shop.

CHAPTER TWENTY-ONE

Chase

EVERY FRIDAY, MR. JENKINS passed out a problem set to a chorus of pre-planned moaning. He challenged us on purpose. The problem sets were always based on the material he'd gone over earlier in the week and usually it took the whole period to complete them. I'd forgotten to warn Lilah to bring her graphing calculator with her to class, but by the time I'd pulled out mine for us both to share, she'd already slid a piece of paper across the table. It was the problem set, completed with all of her work shown step by step.

"How'd you do it so fast?" Connor asked with wide eyes.

She bent down to retrieve a textbook from her backpack. "He posted the questions on the class website last night."

"Sweet," Connor said, grabbing his pencil so he could

start copying down her answers without hesitation.

"You know we're supposed to work on them together," I said, daring a glance in her direction.

She was flipping through her physics book, turning to the section on electricity and magnetism that we weren't due to start for another two weeks.

"Yeah, well, I'm not really a group project kind of girl, especially when I can solve them all on my own."

I smirked and shook my head. "Almost all of them..."

Her pale eyes slid to me as she tried to gauge whether or not I was bluffing.

"You got number one wrong. It's okay to ask for help—"

Her brows furrowed as she reached across the table and yanked the problem set out of Connor's hand.

"Hey! I was copyi—er, reviewing that!"

"It's not wrong," she protested, scanning over her work.

"You forgot to count the energy lost to friction. It said we could neglect air resistance, not friction."

She scanned the word problem, groaned, and then reached for her pencil so she could start erasing her work. Connor followed suit, and soon Lilah and I were working together to tackle the problems. I would read the problem, figure out which equation to use, and Lilah would confirm my guess or argue her point. Connor offered overenthusiastic encouragement and copied down whatever we wrote. Even without his help, we were the first group to finish.

Mr. Jenkins studied us over the rim of his glasses as we dropped the papers on his desk.

"Stay quiet while the other students finish," he said before going back to grading.

Lilah returned to her textbook as soon as we reached

our seats, but I was too anxious to keep working; there were only fifteen minutes until the weekend.

Apparently Connor felt the same way because he leaned forward and tried to get Lilah's attention across the table.

"Psst, Lilah."

She ignored him and flipped to the next page in her textbook.

"Lilah, I have two questions for you."

She finally glanced up.

"What's your favorite color?"

She smirked. "The color of avidly anticipating your second question."

I laughed under my breath, but Connor pushed on full steam ahead.

"That's not a color. Why did you leave Blackwater?"

Idiot. I kicked him under the table. He'd been begging me for details about Lilah all week. He'd felt like everyone was in on a secret but him. I would have told him had I known he'd try and go straight to the source. I turned to Lilah, expecting to find her completely shut down, but she shrugged off his question like it meant nothing at all.

"It's a shame," she said, tapping the physics textbook with her pencil. "A part of me hoped you would be better at asking questions than you are at answering them."

The bell rang and before I could try to smooth over Connor's mistake, Lilah stuffed her textbook into her bag and walked out without looking back.

CHAPTER TWENTY-TWO

Lilah

CONNOR HAD A lot to learn. He wanted to know the secret every student was whispering about in the hallways, but he wouldn't be learning it from me. Secrets aren't projected over loud speakers; they're whispered in the hallways between classes like a commodity. A secret for a secret. Had he approached me in the hallway before class with a good trade, maybe I would have told him. I could have regaled him with the whole wretched tale, but I knew he didn't have any good secrets. It'd be a waste of memories. He'd have to just ask someone else.

As soon as I walked out of physics, I headed for the closest exit and pulled my headphones out of my backpack.

"Lilah!"

Chase's voice boomed over the chatter near the parking lot. Students were waiting for their rides to pick them up at the curb, but I cut through without stopping.

"Lilah!"

I cursed under my breath and turned in time to see Chase running to catch up to me. He'd left his group of friends behind—two baseball guys and a few cheerleaders—and they stood watching him with shocked expressions. I crossed my arms over my chest as my gaze met Kimberly's. For a brief second, I wasn't sure what expression I saw behind her crystal blue eyes, but then she smiled and offered me a small wave.

I waved back just as Chase fell into my line of sight. His unruly blond hair was standing up in every direction, his chest hidden beneath a fitted white t-shirt. His eyes were locked on me and his smile—the smile that unwound my world—was effortlessly genuine. I'd sat next to him for the last forty-five minutes and I'd successfully avoided it. Now, it was too late.

"What are you doing?" I asked, my tone harder than I'd intended.

"Walking home with you." He tugged on his backpack, repositioning it on his shoulders. "No practice on Fridays."

"Your friends probably aren't happy about you ditching them," I said, turning toward the sidewalk, knowing he'd fall into place beside me.

"Well you're my oldest friend, so you get top priority."

"Priority?" I asked with a quizzical brow.

"Yup. Premium walking-home privileges. It's a coveted spot."

"Well, I'd hate to take that away from someone who actually wants it," I said, pressing play on my iPod.

I couldn't hear his reply, but my music wasn't loud enough to drown out his smile.

CHAPTER TWENTY-THREE

Lilah

I DIDN'T WANT to walk home with Chase. I didn't want to stand at the threshold of my room, staring at his door in the darkness. The night before, I'd almost knocked to ask him if he needed someone to talk to, if he still missed his mom as much as I missed mine, but that hallway was blocked with the barbed wires of our past and I couldn't conjure the courage to step over them.

"Is that what you're wearing?" Ashley asked, tugging me out of my thoughts. I sat in her room, watching her get ready for the party I'd grudgingly agreed to attend with her and Trent.

I glanced down at my skinny jeans and Black Keys t-shirt. The t-shirt was snug and fit my frame well. I hadn't thought about the party when I'd gotten dressed that morning before school, but it would have to do.

I looked up at Ashley and shrugged. "It's not like I have time to go home and change."

She reached into her closet and pulled out a black leather miniskirt. "Here, put this on at least."

I caught it as she tossed it over to me and decided that caving and wearing the skirt would be easier than fighting about it. I had to pick my battles with her. She'd already been annoyed when I'd told her I was done taking Molly.

"Where'd you get those pills anyway?" I asked as I unzipped my jeans and slipped into the skirt. I wished it had another inch or two of fabric, but I just tugged it down a sliver and then knotted my shirt above my waist so it looked like an intentional outfit. I ran my hand across the sliver of exposed stomach, fighting an intrusive curiosity: what would it feel like to have Chase's hands there?

"I don't remember. I got them a while back. I'm still going to take one even if you aren't," she threatened as she layered on her mascara in the bathroom mirror.

"Be my guest," I said, making a mental note to keep track of her at the party.

"Any updates about Chase? Does his holiness even bother acknowledging your presence?"

"He mostly keeps to himself," I lied.

She dropped her mascara on the counter and then spun around to face me. She'd redone the pink streaks in her blonde hair earlier that day so they were even more vibrant. I focused on them as she spoke.

"I just don't see how you can live across the hall from him. That would be so weird."

Her words were scraping at scabs I wasn't ready to pick. "Whatever. Are you almost ready? Trent is picking us up in like five minutes."

She smacked her lips and reached back to grab a bag of

little white pills from her purse.

"Time to roll," she said before popping two into her mouth.

I watched her swallow them and tried to fight away thoughts of my mom clawing their way to the front of my mind. Why was it so hard for her to turn down a high? I watched Ashley inhale those pills and I felt no desire to join her. If it was so easy for me to turn them down, why could my mother never manage it?

"Last chaaaaaance," Ashley announced, shaking the little bag. I had to fight the urge to grab it and flush the pills down the toilet. "You sure you don't want some?"

I pushed off her bed and headed for the door. "Positive."

"All right, Miss Priss."

My phone buzzed in my hand before I could respond.

Trent: Outside.

Perfect.

"Trent just got here. I'm going to head down," I said, leaving her room before she could follow after me. I headed outside to find Trent sitting behind the wheel of his silver Camry. His friend Duncan sat in the passenger seat beside him. Duncan had a thing with Ashley—or as she explained it, they "liked hooking up with each other while drunk."

"You look sexy, babe." Trent whistled as I hopped into the backseat. Duncan twisted around to inspect me and his smile made me want to gag. He reminded me of a snake with his sunken cheekbones and chin that tapered off at a sharp angle.

"Yeah Calloway," Duncan added. "You really came

into your own since you left."

His dark gaze had a way of making my skin crawl.

I shifted my gaze to Trent and took him in. A tattered t-shirt covered his thin build and his jet-black hair hung low over his forehead, purposely disheveled. He flashed me a crooked smile and his dark eyes held mine.

"Where's Ashley?" he asked with an arched brow, tapping his fingers on the steering wheel impatiently.

I shrugged. "She was supposed to head out right after me."

Duncan rubbed his hands together greedily. "She better bring the Molly with her. I hooked up with Sasha last week and I can't face her unless I get fucked up."

I ignored him and turned to stare out the window. I chewed on the inside of my cheek and found myself wishing I was with another group of people—or better yet, at home reading with Harvey.

A few minutes later, Ashley finally fell into the backseat with two water bottles in her hands.

"Sorry, I had to raid my parent's liquor cabinet. Sasha always runs out," she said, shaking the water bottles, which I then realized were full of vodka, not water.

"Nice," Duncan complimented, grabbing one of the bottles and taking a swig.

Trent met my eyes in his review mirror and gave me a small smile. I shrugged and smiled back, praying he'd be an ally tonight. If Duncan and Ashley were both drunk and high, they'd be a handful.

Sasha Olsen was a junior at our school with very rich, very neglectful parents. They left her every few months to jet off to some exotic location, and she used the opportunity to throw parties at their ranch out on the edge of town. Trent explained that she'd stepped up her game even more while I'd been away. There was usually a bonfire and a few kegs, and unlike other parties around our town, Sasha's parties weren't exclusive to one clique. Everyone at our school was welcome.

When we pulled up along the line of cars that were parked outside of her ranch, I knew the party was going to be huge. There was nearly a quarter mile of cars leading up to the front drive. The four of us started the trek up to her house, passing tipsy teenagers as we went.

Trent fell into place next to me, skimming his hand along the bare skin between my shirt and my skirt. His touch was warm, but it reminded me of Chase. *Why? Why? Why was he suddenly so impossible to forget?* I tried to push him out of my mind, but I knew he'd be at the party.

The music from the house grew louder as we made our way up the cobblestone path. Trent kept me tucked close to his side as he greeted people we passed.

"What's up?" I asked, glancing down to his hand clamped around my waist.

He flashed me a confident grin. "You just look so good, I don't want you getting swooped up by another guy."

I hadn't been expecting such an honest answer from him and for some reason it didn't sit well with me. I didn't want to date Trent, I hardly knew him, but giving in was easier than fighting him, and pissing him off would mean I had no ride home.

We stepped inside and he bent down to whisper in my ear.

"You want a drink?"

In that moment I glanced across the room and made eye contact with Chase leaning against the kitchen counter. He was surrounded by friends, but his hazel eyes were on me and his brows were cocked in question.

My first instinct was to shove Trent so far away from me that he'd never come back, but I just stood there, completely still, waiting for life to continue as planned. It felt like we hung there staring at each other for hours, until finally Kimberly nudged Chase's side and pressed up onto her tiptoes to whisper in his ear.

Seeing her there felt like a punch to the gut and I had to fight the urge to bend forward and grip my knees until the sensation passed. I counted to three. One. *Chase and I used to be friends but we aren't any more.* Two. *Kimberly was there for him when I couldn't be.* Three. *I'm here with Trent and he's here with her. Done.*

"Did you hear me Lilah? Do you want a drink?" Trent asked again.

I shook my head. "Want to go out back?" I asked, turning toward our small band of misfits.

Ashley and Duncan were taking turns sipping from the vodka water bottles. They'd be completely wasted in thirty minutes or less.

"You should get some water, Ashley."

"Thank you, *mother*, but I'll be fine." She rolled her eyes and turned toward Duncan so he could sweep her up into a sloppy kiss. I wanted to throttle the pair of them, but I swallowed past my annoyance just as a hand touched my shoulder. It was too strong and too familiar to be Trent's.

"Lil, can we talk for a second?"

I turned around to see Chase standing beside Trent, towering over him by a few inches. I hated seeing them standing so close together. It was impossible not to compare them and I knew Trent would never stack up. Chase might have been more handsome with his classic golden boy looks, but it wasn't about that. Chase was my childhood, my memories, and my happiness—things I worried I'd never get back.

"Lil?" Trent repeated my nickname, testing it out for the first time with a furrowed brow.

Chase smirked. "I've called her that since we were kids," he clarified, letting go of my shoulder at the same time Trent broke his connection with my waist.

"I was about to get Lilah a drink," Trent said, crossing his arms over his chest.

Chase narrowed his eyes on him for a moment. "Perfect timing then, thanks buddy."

I nodded at Trent, unable to find words to mask the awkwardness.

We moved past Trent and started heading toward the backyard. I could see the bonfire through the windows and just before I pushed open the back door, I saw Chase's reflection in the glass. His face was focused, sharp. His eyes held none of the humor they usually did.

Four massive logs sat on the ground, framing the bonfire. They'd be completely covered with partygoers later, but for now they were empty and waiting for us. He held the door for me and then pressed his hand to the small of my back to lead me toward the fire. One of Chase's fingers slipped past the fabric of my shirt and sent a shiver down my spine. I inhaled a deep breath and sidestepped out of his grasp to sit down on one of the massive logs, at once relieved and sad to lose the connection.

I stretched my legs and crossed my feet as Chase took a seat beside me.

Silence hung between us as I waited for him to speak first. When he didn't, I bit the bullet.

"Why did you want to talk to me?"

I peered over to see him watching the bonfire. The shadow from the flames danced across his features.

"Why are you with Trent?"

"I'm not."

He grunted in disbelief.

"We're not dating. He just wants to sleep with me. Not that it's any of your business."

Chase cursed under his breath and leaned forward to rest his forearms on his legs. His hands were clasped together so tightly his knuckles turned white.

"You shouldn't ask questions if you can't handle the answers," I spat with narrowed eyes.

He shook his head. "He's not enough for you."

"I'm not asking for anything more."

"You should be."

I leaned forward to match his posture and we let the silence wrap around us once again. It'd been so long since we'd just sat together. It felt like I was taking a trip down memory lane and the comfort pulled questions out of me that I hadn't thought about for years.

"Why aren't you as messed up as I am, Chase? After everything that's happened?"

The edge of Chase's mouth curved skyward. "You're not messed up."

I looked away.

He continued. "I decided a long time ago to just live in the moment, to forget the past and just exist in this"—he pointed to the ground—"exact moment. Believe me, it's not easy. I have a dad that can't sober up to raise me and you had a mom that couldn't sober up to raise you."

I bit my lip, listening to his words and wondering if I could ever apply them to my life. "We're a regular afterschool special."

He finally peered over at me. "Yeah well, this is life. Not everyone gets a happy ending."

I laughed sadly. "So then why do you insist on trying to give me one?"

He took a moment to answer my question, but when he did, I listened to every syllable as carefully as possible. "It'd be a damn shame if all this turmoil was for nothing. Don't you think?"

I stared into the fire and nodded, letting his words sink in before I spoke up again. "What if I'm past the point of return?"

His hazel eyes scanned down my face. "You aren't. You just need a little help."

I rolled my eyes. "And you think you'll be the person to help me?"

He smirked and leaned in so that I caught a whiff of his cologne. "I can definitely do a better job than Trent."

My eyes fell to his lips as he leaned in, dangerously close. Half of his features were illuminated by the firelight and half of them were cast in shadows. It was a dangerous image: Chase dipping into the darkness to help pull me to the light.

"What are you doing?" I asked with a shaky breath. I wanted him to kiss me, to finish leaning forward and press his lips to mine. It would have stolen my breath, I knew it.

"Hey Chase, Kimberly needs your help," a voice called from the back door, interrupting our moment. I glanced up to see Connor standing in the doorway, waiting for Chase to get up. His eyes shifted to me and he shrugged apologetically.

Of course Kimberly needed him.

I closed my eyes and built reality back up around me. Any hope of Chase and I ending up together was based in delusion.

"Duty calls," I said, pushing up off the bench and

walking away from the bonfire. It was the first real moment I'd had with Chase in two years and I'd been so close to letting him in again, so close to closing the gap between us and kissing him senseless. But Chase had said it best: this was our story and happy endings are few and far between. We'd forever be moving in opposite directions—after all, he was the golden boy, and I was the lost girl.

CHAPTER TWENTY-FOUR

Chase

I WATCHED LILAH go back inside and felt her slipping away even faster than before. When she'd arrived with Trent, I'd moved toward her without a purpose. I'd touched her hand, and I'd mentioned her old nickname like I was trying to jog her memory.

I'd managed to pull her away from Trent for a few minutes and I knew I was getting through to her, but it wasn't enough. I needed more time.

I stood and shoved my fingers through my hair, restraining an annoyed groan.

"Were you about to get it on with Lilah?" Connor asked with a smirk.

I shoved him, hard. "You're pushing it."

His eyes widened and he held his palms up in surrender; I'd never once yelled at him like that. "Whoa, whatever man. Just come help. Kimberly is drunk and throwing up in the bathroom. She keeps asking for you."

When I walked inside the house I scanned the room for Lilah, but she wasn't in the living room, which meant she was probably off somewhere with Trent. I balled my hands and followed Connor.

We found Kimberly in the master bathroom, leaning over the toilet with her blonde hair spilling out around her. When she heard us walk in, she turned toward me with a dopey smile.

"Chase! You came!" she exclaimed before breaking into a fit of laughter. Brian sat behind her on the lip of the bathtub, wrestling with himself. He watched her with concerned eyes, which were magnified by the fact that he'd had a thing for Kimberly for as long as I could remember.

"How much did you drink tonight, Kimberly?" I asked.

"Actual shots or just the little ones?" She giggled before starting to tick off drinks on her fingers. When she passed one hand, I shook my head.

"Brian, do you think you could take her home?" I asked.

His eyes lit up and he shot off the bathtub. "Yeah, definitely."

She pushed her bottom lip out. "No. No. I want you to take me!"

Brian stepped back toward the bathtub, wounded by her rejection. I'd known from the beginning it was a mistake to date Kimberly. Each time something started between us, I'd try to tell myself I had feelings for her. I was dumb enough to use her as a distraction, hoping my feelings would eventually catch up to hers, but they never did. She was smart, and gorgeous, and kind, but she wasn't Lilah.

It was time to end it for good.

"I'm not leaving yet. I need to find Lilah."

Kimberly wasn't a fool; even in her drunken state she caught what I meant.

She let her bottom lip slide past her teeth and glanced back toward Brian. "Okay, Brian would you mind taking me home?" She smiled. "Pretty please?"

Brian, unscathed from the earlier snubbing, looked like he'd just won the lottery ten times over. "Sure! Yeah, let me go get my car. I'll meet you guys out front."

He shot out of the bathroom, leaving me alone with Kimberly. I stepped forward to help her stand up and she threw her weight against me. I pulled her arm around my shoulder and wrapped my hand around her waist so I could carry some of her weight. The second we walked out of the bathroom, she started giggling again.

"I should have known nothing had changed. You love Lilah *soooo* much. It's so cute. You know she's really nice and she tries to hide with all the black hair, but she's still so pretty. I wonder if she'd want to be my friend again." She kept rambling and I couldn't help but smile down at her. At least she was a bubbly drunk.

We'd made it midway through the living room when I looked up and spotted Lilah standing with Trent against the wall. His arm was caging her in on one side as he leaned down to talk to her, but she wasn't watching him. Her eyes were locked on me and Kimberly. She watched Kimberly smile up at me and then her gaze fell to my hands wrapped around Kimberly's waist.

She pinched her eyes closed as she processed what she thought she was seeing. When she opened them again, they were a shade darker and narrowed in anger. I watched her lift up onto her toes, wrap her hand around Trent's neck, pull his face toward her, and kiss him. He'd been in the middle of a sentence, but she kissed him hard and stole the rest of his words.

CHAPTER TWENTY-FIVE

Lilah

I DON'T KNOW why I kissed Trent. In the past, seeing Chase with Kimberly had lit a dull flame in the pit of my stomach, but now it was a wildfire, burning me from the inside out. Seeing his arm around her, seeing her smile up at him, seeing their features perfectly complement one another was enough to send me over the edge. I pulled Trent's face down to mine and tried to channel every ounce of rage into a kiss, but it didn't work. His breath tasted like stale tobacco and when I closed my eyes, I still saw Chase's hazel gaze staring back at me.

I pulled back and took a deep breath.

When I glanced over to where Chase had just been standing, he was gone. He'd left with Kimberly.

Good.

They could go fuck each other somewhere else.

"I like when you take charge," Trent said, dipping his head lower and kissing the side of my neck.

His lips swept across my skin, dipping toward the neckline of my t-shirt. My hands wrapped around his biceps as I tried to force my attention onto the guy in front of me instead of the one who'd just left.

"Guys, guys, guys." Duncan stumbled toward us, his eyes dilated wide. "Ashley is freaking out."

"Whatever, tell her to chill," Trent groaned.

"No man, it's serious. She's really bugging."

"What do you mean?" I asked.

Duncan led us to the restroom Kimberly and Chase had left a few minutes prior. Ashley was sitting on the ground with sweat covering her forehead. Her dilated eyes matched Duncan's, and when I felt her forehead, she was burning up.

"Trent, go get some water from the kitchen."

Ashley was clutching her knees and grinding her teeth. I tried to get her attention, to get her to focus on me, but her eyes were darting in every direction but mine.

"Ashley, are you okay?" I snapped my fingers. "Ashley, focus."

"I don't feel good," she murmured so softly I could hardly hear her.

"Do you think you can throw up?" I asked, trying to think of the fastest method to get all the crap out of her system.

"No. No," she cried. "I don't want to throw up. Don't make me throw up."

She didn't sound like herself and the way her eyes were darting around the room was starting to scare me.

Trent rushed back into the bathroom with a glass of water. I gripped the back of Ashley's head and forced most of the liquid down her throat. She didn't want to drink it, but her body was dehydrated and even if she wasn't my best friend, I wasn't going to let her die from being a complete idiot.

The water settled in her stomach for a moment, and then she twisted toward the toilet and threw it all up.

"Good," I said, holding her hair back as a wave of déjà vu swept me back in time to my house before my mom had left.

When I was seven, there were a few months when my mother must have started to realize her addiction was no longer manageable. She tried to hide her increasing dependence on alcohol, but I'd come home from school and find her in the bathroom, throwing up and mumbling things I couldn't discern. I'd hold back her hair—the same way I now held Ashley's—and wonder if this was what other seven-year-olds did when they got home from school.

"I got her some more water," Duncan said, stumbling back into the bathroom.

I held the glass of water to her lips again so she could take small sips. If she could absorb some of it before throwing up, she'd start to feel better.

I'd been around people like Ashley in Austin, other kids who liked to push their limits. I'd even done it myself from time to time, hoping to find the same solace my mom had found. I wanted to feel what she'd felt. I wanted to know what was so appealing about getting so far out of your head you couldn't recognize yourself any more. I was starting to think maybe she and I weren't wired the same. To me, the high was never worth the fall.

The guys eventually abandoned us and Ashley leaned against the toilet dry heaving. I couldn't leave her yet and I was tired of replaying shitty memories, so I scanned the bathroom for something to distract me.

There were crosses everywhere, the kind you find at small country boutiques with ribbons and bedazzled gemstones. A small collection hung directly behind the toilet, which seemed like an odd location to display faith, but I didn't dwell on that fact. Instead, I turned for the medicine cabinet.

Medicine cabinets are a veritable trove of pharmaceutical secrets, but it takes a trained eye to discern the juicy from the mundane. A thyroid medication could treat an underactive thyroid, or it could be mommy's favorite weight loss pill. The devil was in the details. I turned to check on Ashley, but she wasn't watching as I popped the door open and peered inside.

Sasha's parents had a twenty-acre ranch, a 6,000 square foot mansion, and a four-car garage, but they also had a neat little row of pill bottles lining their medicine cabinet.

Viagra.

Erectile dysfunction.

Ephedren.

Illegal weight loss supplement.

Finesteride.

Male pattern baldness.

Xanax.

A benzo for days when the four-car garage just isn't enough.

Valium.

For when the Xanax isn't enough.

It wasn't until later as I laid down to go to sleep that I remembered Sasha's mom was the journalist who'd written the exposé about my mother for our town's newspaper. It was a page-long article highlighting the darkest points in my mother's pitiful life, and it was printed in the same newspaper that later ran her abbreviated obituary.

I wondered if Sasha's mom had come clean about her family's own dependencies in that article, or if all 2,000 words had been reserved for my mother's demons. Maybe she knew as well as I did that there's power in shining light on other people's secrets; it makes it that much easier to hide yours in the shadows.

CHAPTER TWENTY-SIX

Lilah

THE NEXT MORNING I made my way downstairs to find Chase and my dad in the kitchen making breakfast. Chase was scrambling eggs, and my dad was mixing pancake batter. I hated having Chase there; his casual presence seemed wrong in every way.

"Morning Lil," Chase said as my dad tipped back on his heels to kiss me on the top of my head.

"Morning," I responded weakly. I'd already seen everything I needed to on the way down the stairs and his affinity for low-slung sweatpants was starting to annoy me.

"You know one day I'm going to go in my closet and find that all of my t-shirts have disappeared," my dad noted with a smile.

I'd started stealing shirts out of his closet when I was younger and I'd never stopped. They were old and worn and they smelled like him. I wasn't sure why I still wore them, but I had no plans of stopping.

"You can borrow some of mine," Chase whispered so my dad couldn't hear over the sound of the whisk.

I ignored him, trying hard not to imagine getting to sleep with Chase's scent wrapped around me.

Once they finished making breakfast, we took seats around the table and I tore into the pancakes, appreciating every maple syrup-covered bite.

"What do you have planned for today?" my dad asked the table.

"I think I'm going to work on the garden," I replied.

He nodded. "It's a good day for it. We could clear some of the beds and then head up to the store for some planting soil."

"I can help," Chase offered.

I was staring down at my eggs, but I could see him watching me out of the corner of my eye. Gardening was the one thing my mom and I had done together before she passed away. My most vivid memory of her being happy was when we gardened, so to bring Chase into that equation seemed like I was somehow stomping on her memory.

I tightened my hold on my fork as they waited for me to respond. I couldn't say no. It would raise too many questions and I didn't feel like explaining my convoluted reasoning to anyone.

"Actually, I just remembered I have some homework I need to finish. Maybe I'll start on the garden next week."

CHAPTER TWENTY-SEVEN

Chase

AS FAR BACK as I could remember, my dad had always worked on Sundays. It was his day to finish repairs and catch up on paperwork, but when I pulled up into a vacant parking spot in front of the shop, the lights were off and the door was locked. I popped the lock and strolled inside to find evidence of his recent departure. There was an empty pizza box with a receipt taped to the front. It was only two days old, so at least I knew he was alive. He couldn't return my calls, but he could order a pizza.

I tossed the empty box into the trash along with a few empty beer cans, and then checked the office's computer for recent repair requests. He'd always kept them on a simple excel sheet. His usual turnaround time for a job was two weeks so he'd have time to order any necessary parts. The most recent jobs on the excel sheet were all a month or two old and not a single one of them had been finished.

I printed out the sheet of unfinished repair requests and pushed my way into the back room. Tools and appliances littered the floor. A box of mismatched parts lay forgotten in the corner. I kicked it aside and started clearing out a workspace. The repair requests weren't complicated; two blenders, a washing machine, and a refrigerator were on the top of the list. I assessed the damage and started to draw up an order form for parts. My dad had been ordering from the same distributor for the last ten years and I knew they wouldn't question my scratchy signature at the bottom of the order form.

After I'd managed to get the recent repairs in order, I tore open the stack of deliveries behind the counter. My dad had managed to carry the packages inside, but he hadn't taken the time to open a single one.

I took inventory of the parts and matched them with the appliances in the back room. I spent my entire day trying to catch up on the work my dad was obviously neglecting, and as I locked up in the dark, I knew my effort was in vain. I could come back every Sunday, but until my dad got his act together, the shop would suffer. There was no point trying to fight it.

CHAPTER TWENTY-EIGHT

Chase

THAT NIGHT I passed up invitations from Connor and Brian so I could stay at Lilah's house. I sat in her backyard on the swing beneath the oak tree that faced the back of the house. It was hung for a child, too low to the ground for me to go very high. I used my foot to push off the ground, rocking the swing back and then letting gravity carry me forward again. Harvey lay on the grass at the foot of the tree, content to study me as I studied the yard.

The dormant flowerbeds scattered across the yard were as much a part of my childhood as they were Lilah's. I'd beg and beg to taste the strawberries every season and one time, when I'd assumed Lilah was busy across the yard, I'd reached down and yanked the biggest one off the vine. Just as the sweet juice slipped across my tongue, the sharp sting of cold water hit the side of my face. Lilah had turned the hose on me and I'd learned my lesson.

I sat out on the swing until it started to rain, but I didn't care. It was the lazy kind of rain that couldn't catch me on the swing; the fat drops were too slow. I kept pushing myself back and forth, letting my mind wander to my mom. It'd been raining the last time I'd talked to her. It was the night of the annual summer carnival up at the school. My dad and I were leaving early to help with setup and I'd almost left the house without telling her bye. I thought about that a lot lately, how it'd been such a fluke. She'd caught me at the bottom of the stairs, just as I was about to walk out the door.

"Chase, make sure your dad doesn't lift anything too heavy. He threw his back out last year setting up the dunking booth."

I rolled my eyes and nodded, anxious to get to my friends, but she caught my arm.

"Be good," she said, tapping the brim of my baseball cap with her finger.

I smiled, despite the cap falling down to cover my eyes.

It wasn't an official goodbye. She hadn't told me she'd loved me, but I didn't focus on that. I knew how much she loved me. She'd told me every day.

For months after that night, the what-ifs had kept me awake at night. *What if she'd never gone back home from the carnival? What if the ambulance had arrived faster?*

I wasn't the only one battling a losing fight against what-ifs. My dad had started drinking the day of the funeral and he'd never stopped. Death can do strange things to people. It can turn a man I'd admired my whole life into a guy I'd avoid if I saw him on the street.

Elaine Calloway had stolen both of my parents from me. Maybe I should have hated Lilah for being a part of her, but I couldn't. Lilah was good. She was beautiful and she created beauty with her garden. Out of such terrible things, the muck and the mud, Lilah had come to be. Life had done its best to stomp her back into dust, but I wouldn't let it happen.

Her light flickered off in her room, replaced with the glow from her lamp. I watched her silhouette move in front of the window and I realized that whatever love my mom had held for Elaine was the same love that tied me to Lilah.

I pushed off the swing as rain continued to hammer down around me. Harvey hopped up and followed me as I headed inside, up the stairs, and toward Lilah's room. Her door was cracked open and through the space between her door and the doorframe, I could see her reading on her bed. I knocked gently and then pushed the door open a crack. Harvey pushed it open even more and ran straight for her, resting his damp snout next to her pillow.

She smiled and flipped her book down onto her chest to mark her page.

"He's all wet," she said, glancing over at me.

I rested my head on the doorframe. "We were outside when the storm started."

She nodded, dragging her hand up Harvey's snout, over his head and behind his ears.

I thought of asking her about the book she was reading, but I had something I needed to do.

I turned and headed into the room across the hall, closing the door after Harvey had followed me inside. It was late, but that didn't stop me from pulling my phone out of my pocket to call my dad. I figured he might be awake, but after it rang and rang and he still didn't answer, I left a message.

"Hey Dad, this is Chase. I haven't talked to you for a few days so I wanted to catch up and see how you were doing. Everything's good at Lilah's house, but I was wondering if we could go to dinner or something this week. Give me a call back if you get this."

I hung up and stared down at my phone, wondering if he'd ever be sober enough to check that message. *Probably not.* I tightened my fist around the cheap phone and then threw it onto my bed. It bounced off and hit the stack of boxes in the corner, the boxes I tried to avoid.

I bent to retrieve it and caught sight of Elaine's name scrawled in Sharpie across the bottom box. It was there every time I glanced at the boxes, a daily reminder of the woman I hated most in life. I took a pen from my desk and scratched at her name, covering it with angry black strokes until I couldn't read it any more.

She didn't deserve to be remembered, not by me.

CHAPTER TWENTY-NINE

Lilah

LUNCH WAS THE hour that had brought me the most anxiety during my first week back in Blackwater. Our school's cafeteria was small, suffocating, and operated like the English class system. I avoided it at all costs, opting instead to explore my options. The women's bathroom proved quiet, but smelly. The locker room was comfortable, but awkward when the junior girls had to change for P.E. Eventually, I'd stumbled upon the nature center in the back of the school and had fallen in love. None of the other students ventured out there unless they were required to go for a science class. It felt like a hidden gem that only I knew about, my own secret garden.

The school did a terrible job of maintaining it, but that made it even better. The overgrown trees and shrubs concealed me away as I traversed the short path toward the bench I'd designated as my lunch spot since the Friday before. No one knew I was out there—not Ashley or Trent—so when I heard a twig snap behind me, my heart kicked into overdrive. I froze and twisted around to find Chase standing in the clearing behind me, holding his hands up in surrender. His worn jeans and old raglan t-shirt pushed up to his elbows only seemed to enhance his harmlessness.

"Mind if I join you?" he asked before taking a hesitant step forward.

Truthfully, I didn't want company, but he was already there, stepping toward my bench. He'd already infiltrated my secret hideout, so there was no point in pushing him back out. I shrugged and turned for the bench to take a seat.

My ears perked up as I listened to him approach. He stepped around the bench to take a seat beside me, momentarily replacing the scent of nature with his cologne. I gave myself two deep breaths before I forced myself to think of something else, like the field of wildflowers in front of me, overgrown with bright red petals.

"Second week back and you're already breaking rules?" he asked.

I ignored him and pulled out my peanut butter and jelly sandwich.

"Why do you eat lunch out here?" he asked, staring out at the field alongside me.

"So people like you won't talk to me," I answered with a little smile so he'd know I wasn't a total bitch—just enough of one.

He laughed and I fought to keep my gaze off him. "Y'know, my favorite thing about you is your charm. I don't think you get enough credit for how charming you are."

I chewed on my lip, trying to interpret if he was being

sarcastic or not. Either way, I relented.

Tilting my head toward him, I answered, "I don't really want to sit in the cafeteria for an hour every day."

"But your friends are in there," he pointed out, trying to get to the real explanation.

"*Friends* is a relative term," I answered, picking up a small stick from the bench and tossing it out onto the ground.

He smirked. "Yeah, they kind of suck."

"Eff you, those are my friends..." I said with a smirk.

I hadn't talked to any of them since Sasha's party on Saturday. I'd avoided the stoner-tree and Trent's texts. It felt good to have a break from pretending to like people.

"Am I your friend?"

I picked a particularly bright poppy and focused on it like my life depended on it.

"That word never really worked for you," I admitted, feeling my heart rate quicken.

He nodded. "It wasn't enough."

The weight of his words threatened to undo the tiny string that tied my heart together.

"Or it was too much."

"You know, in a lot of ways, I still know you better than anyone," he continued.

I hiked up my brows and turned to face him. His gaze was focused on the flowers, but that grin was ever present.

"Why do you think that?" I asked, curious about why he still felt connected to me after all these years. I was nothing like the girl that he'd known back then.

"I've seen you cry and laugh and throw fits. I've seen you naked," he laughed.

I hated that I blushed when he admitted that, but I was helpless to stop the reaction.

"When I was like seven..." I reasoned, trying to point out the flaw in his thinking.

"Yeah, but I'll bet you still have that little freckle on your left butt cheek," he declared, turning toward me with a sly grin. I decided to play his game.

"And I'll bet you're still the same size down there that you were then."

He tossed his head back and laughed, a loud, rich laugh that tugged at the corners of my mouth.

"It wasn't that long ago that we were best friends. What changed?"

I backpedaled, scared of the guilt creeping its way up my throat. "What are you talking about? Everything changed."

Silence fell after that and I knew I'd hurt him. I never seemed to know how to handle myself around him since my mother's death. Instead of apologizing, I tore off half of my peanut butter and jelly sandwich and held it out to him. It was an apology wedged between two slices of white bread, and he took it.

CHAPTER THIRTY

Lilah

AFTER SCHOOL ON Tuesday, I didn't walk home; I headed in the direction of my mom's old apartment. It was on the other side of Main Street, where the houses were a little smaller and the tenants were more rough around the edges. After she'd left when I was seven, she'd moved into a one-bedroom apartment that smelled like bleach every time I went over to visit on Saturday afternoons. My dad would drop me off at her door, only leaving when he was sure I was safely inside. From there, I had five unsupervised hours with her.

She was never genuinely happy to see me. At the time, I hadn't noticed, too blinded by my own excitement to pick up on the subtle signs. She'd turn on the TV, plant me on the couch, and then go in the other room and talk on the phone or flip through a magazine—anything to avoid me.

A year or two into our Saturday afternoon visits, there

was a knock on her apartment door. I was coloring in the living room and even though I knew I wasn't supposed to, I peered over. There was a man standing at the threshold, pressing the door open with his hand. A cigarette hung between his lips and a scar stretched from his eyelid down to the top of his lip. Small scabs were littered across his cheeks and chin. They looked like the scabs I got when I scratched too much at a mosquito bite. I wondered how he could have managed to get so many bites just as he bent down to grip my mother's neck in his hand.

His cigarette fell to the floor, burning ash into the fake wood as I jumped up to stop him. I wanted to scream at him to leave her alone, but she waved behind her back, warning me away. I clenched my fists, trying to think of what to do. The phone was in the kitchen and I couldn't figure out a way to sneak past without him noticing.

I stood scared and frozen in the living room as he bent low and whispered something only she could hear. She pleaded with him, begging for more time. Then as quickly as he'd arrived, he unwrapped his hand from my mother's neck and left. When she shut the door, I swiveled back to stare at the TV, trying to pretend like the last few minutes had never happened. I picked up my crayon and tried to make my hand stop shaking. She walked into the living room and turned the TV off. The screen faded to black as she told me she had to leave. I asked her over and over again where she was going, but she ignored me as she gathered up my coloring books and shoved them inside my backpack. I wanted to yell at her for crinkling the pages. I wanted her to stop pushing me out the door.

I cradled my toys and snacks in my arms as she gave me orders to sit at the curb of her apartment complex until my dad came to pick me up. Then she disappeared inside her *old red car. There was a giant dent on the back, near the bumper; I stared at it as she pulled away. My bottom lip quivered as the car got smaller and smaller in the distance, but I couldn't cry. If I cried, someone would think I needed help and my mom would get in trouble.*

I had to be a grownup.

For an hour, I sat on the cement with my coloring book unopened on my lap. Any time someone would walk by, I'd tell them that my mom had run back to the apartment to grab something so they wouldn't think I was alone. I was thirsty, but I didn't want to finish my Capri Sun; I wasn't sure how long she'd be gone.

When my father arrived a few hours later, I tried to lie and say my mother had just left, but he wouldn't listen. He was in an absolute rage to find me alone and locked out of my mother's apartment. I begged him not to do anything, but that was the last time he let me go see my mom for a visit. The court rescinded her visitation rights without contest. I wished I knew what had pulled her away from me that day, who or what had been more important than her flesh and blood.

I walked along the sidewalk and then stood across the street from her apartment complex. The building had been worn down when she'd lived there, but it'd become condemnable in the years since. Trash littered the ground and most of the windows were duct-taped and boarded up. Weeds had claimed ownership of the yard a while back but no one seemed to mind. My hand itched to clear them out, but there was no point. If no one cared that they were there, no one would care when they were gone.

I was about to cross the street to get a closer look when I heard my name.

"Lilah?"

I turned to find Trent standing outside of a house a little farther down the street. He was at the top of the stairs, holding the screen door open and narrowing his eyes in confusion. It took me a second to connect the two worlds. I hadn't noticed her apartment the last time I'd been at his house.

"I forgot you lived over here."

He nodded and let the screen door slam closed behind him. We met in the middle of his sidewalk and then turned toward the direction of my mom's old apartment. We stared in silence for a moment and then he spoke up.

"What are you doing on this side of town?"

I glanced at him and then back to the apartment complex. "I'm not really sure."

"You can come inside if you want. My mom's at work and she won't be back for a few hours."

I shook my head. I hadn't walked across town to distract myself with Trent. I'd willingly walked into my past and it felt good to stare it down, to remember that day and realize that my mom had never apologized; hell, she probably didn't even remember it.

I pointed to the curb in front of the apartment. "Do you remember seeing a little girl sitting there years ago? All by herself?"

Trent followed my point and shook his head. "No, but that's not really a place for kids. I've seen some shady shit go down over there."

I stared at the rotted wood and crumbling brick of the complex and remembered the way that man had gripped my mother's neck in the doorway. He could have snapped it in two right in front of me.

Trent was right.

It was no place for a kid.

CHAPTER THIRTY-ONE

November 2009
Blackwater, Texas

CHASE MATTHEWS RAN up the gravel drive just as the setting sun finally disappeared behind the row of houses across the street. He was supposed to have been home already, but the baseball game at the park had run over time. He knew his dad would pop him for being late, but he hoped that if he slipped in unnoticed through the back door, his dad might assume he'd been home all along. He pulled open the screen door and cursed the squeaky hinges. He kicked off his muddy shoes and tiptoed toward the kitchen.

His parents' voices carried over into the hallway, so he pressed against the wall and listened to their conversation, trying to make out if they were talking about him. They were usually so careful; Chase rarely overheard their arguments.

"I don't think you should go. She's a grown woman, Hannah. You can't change her."

"She's my oldest friend, David. I can't just leave her there."

Chase knew right away they were talking about Elaine, Lilah's mom. She'd been getting worse lately, calling his mom at all hours of the night.

His dad cursed under his breath and Chase crept closer to the kitchen. He stayed pinned to the wall as he peered inside. His dad was hunched over, gripping the side of the kitchen island. His mother wound her arms around his waist and rested her head against his back, right between his shoulder blades.

"I promise I won't be gone long. I'll just make sure she's safe and then I'll come right back home."

His dad didn't say anything for the longest time, but then he nodded and wrapped his hands around hers. "Hurry back. I'll finish dinner and we'll wait to eat until you get home."

She kissed him quickly and then grabbed her keys from the counter. When she rounded the doorway and saw Chase standing there, she tilted her head to the side.

"You need to go wash up," she said, licking her thumb and wiping his cheek where dirt was caked from playing baseball outside all day.

"Can I come with you?" he asked. He didn't know where she was going, but he didn't like the idea of her seeing Elaine. She was always protecting Elaine, but who was protecting her?

His mom cupped his chin and bent down to kiss his cheek. Soon she wouldn't have to bend at all; he was nearly her height and growing faster by the day. He couldn't wait for the day he could tease her about being shorter than him.

"I need you to go help your father with dinner," she said before whispering, "He's helpless without you."

He smiled and shook his head before she moved past him, toward the door.

"Love you. Be good," she called back.

He moved after her, holding the screen door open and watching her walk toward her car. The motion-sensor light above the garage kicked on as she closed her car door. Her engine revved and he was left with a sinking feeling in the pit of his stomach.

Even at thirteen, Chase knew Elaine was a bad lady. She'd left Lilah and she'd leave his mom too. One day.

CHAPTER THIRTY-TWO

Chase

TEN DAYS. LILAH and I walked to school together for ten days before she finally paused her music. I was running late thanks to a missed alarm. I threw on my shoes and ran out the door, prepared to have to book it to catch up to Lilah, but she was still at the end of the driveway, fidgeting with her shoes.

She stood as I approached and I noticed her headphones were still in place, but there was no music playing, at least none that I could hear.

We started to walk together in silence. We passed her neighbors' houses and I tried to come up with something interesting to say, something so good she would have to take her headphones out to listen.

"Seems like Harvey likes to sleep with you more than me now."

That didn't even garner a nod.

"We have our first scrimmage of the season tomorrow. It's against Oak Hill."

She pulled her iPod out of her pocket and I knew I was losing traction. That's when Mr. Hill stepped out of his house and headed for his car. He was a lawyer in town who rented out space in the old town hall. Rumor had it he would have to close his practice soon.

"Have you heard that Mr. Hill might have to close his practice? He's been telling people there's not enough work."

Lilah glanced over to watch him slide into his black Lexus and then shook her head. "That's not why he's closing up shop."

I narrowed my eyes.

"He's having an affair with his receptionist," she said matter-of-factly.

"What? How do you know that? You haven't even been in town that long."

She shrugged. "I keep my eyes open."

We turned toward Main Street and I narrowed my eyes, trying to work out her accusation. I'd never heard about an affair. Mr. Hill and his wife had been married for something like thirty years. It didn't make sense.

"Who told you ab—"

She sighed and pulled out her headphones. "No one *told* me anything. I saw them in the window of his office the other morning. It wasn't that hard to connect the dots. It's the closing of his practice that I haven't been able to work out. I think his wife has something to do with it."

I reached for her arm and pulled us to a stop. "Wait. Were you snooping?"

She rolled her eyes. "I don't call it that. Snooping implies that I went out of my way to find out Mr. Hill's secrets. In reality, he was flaunting his affair for anyone to see. I just happened to be at the right place at the right time."

She pulled her arm out of my grip and kept walking. I ran to catch up to her. She seemed so sure of herself, not like someone embarrassed to have stumbled upon an affair.

"Does that happen often? You being in the right place at the right time?"

She smirked. "Sort of."

"What else do you know?"

Her bright eyes slid to me, alight with excitement. "I've been back in Blackwater for two weeks and the things I know could turn this entire town on its head."

"Like what?"

She pointed to a nondescript blue house we were passing on the left. "It's a lot of little things, like that woman that lives there. Mrs. Peterson, right? She steals roses from her neighbor's garden, and Mr. Jenner goes through his next door neighbor's trash."

I stared at the houses as we passed them, wondering if Lilah was telling the truth.

She continued, "We're all consumed with the petty drama, the minor stuff settled right up at the top, like roses and trash. Not many people realize how easy it is to dig a little deeper."

She sounded like she knew from experience.

"You're saying there are bigger secrets? Like what?"

The curl of her lips slowly faded to a straight line as she shrugged.

"Things people would prefer to keep buried."

CHAPTER THIRTY-THREE

Lilah

THE WARNING BELL rang through the hallway, indicating that I had less than a minute to make it across the school for physics. They gave us five minutes to get from one period to the next and I'd thought I'd snub my nose at the establishment by attempting to use the restroom. *Mistake*. I shoved my physics textbook into my backpack and slammed my locker closed. I spun on my heel, prepared to make a run for it, when I nearly ran straight into Ashley.

She laughed. "Sorry, I was calling your name but you didn't hear me."

I smiled, already moving in the direction of my physics class. "Sorry. I'm kind of in a hurry."

Her smile fell. "Oh, it's cool. I just wanted to see if you had plans for this weekend. I think Trent is going to lift some stuff from his mom's boyfriend's stash."

I withheld a cringe. "Actually, I'll probably just stick

close to home this weekend. Binge on Netflix and do that history report I've been putting off."

In truth, I wanted to start working on my garden.

"Sounds fun, except for the fact that Chase will be there." She made a fake gagging motion. "Yeah he's hot, but he's such a goody two-shoes."

"He's not that bad," I shrugged, taking another step back.

"I'm sorry, are you on crack? He's one of the *chosen* people."

Students rushed around us trying to get to class before the tardy bell, but Ashley wasn't the least bit preoccupied by the threat of detention.

"Listen, I gotta get to class. I'll call you later."

Before she could reply, I took off. I knew I looked like a dork running with my backpack jostling around, but I fully embraced it. Our school had zero tolerance for tardiness. Every day, the principal reiterated over morning announcements that being tardy would land you in detention, no exceptions.

I rounded the corner into the science wing and was two feet from the door when the final bell rang, marking my doom with its shrill sound. Mr. Jenkins stood behind his desk prepared to start class, and I knew there was no hope. He'd see me as soon as I walked into the room.

"OH MY GOD. WOULD YOU LOOK AT THAT?!"

Chase was standing by the windows with his hands cupped around his eyes like binoculars. He pressed closer to the glass and stared up at the sky as if he was watching a meteor hurl its way toward earth. All the students jumped out of their seats and ran to get a closer look, and I jumped on the opportunity. Mr. Jenkins yelled at everyone to sit back down and I crept slowly around the edge of the room, trying to slip past him undetected.

"What are you talking about Chase?" one girl asked. "I don't see anything."

"Yeah, nothing's there," another classmate chimed in.

"What?! You don't see it? It's humongous!" Chase exclaimed, pointing wildly toward the sky.

"Chase, you idiot," Connor said, slapping him on the shoulder. "It's just a cloud."

"Yeah, but it's not every day you see a cumulus!"

Mr. Jenkins clapped twice and the sound echoed around the room like brass cymbals.

"That's enough! Nice try Mr. Matthews, but one more distraction like that and you'll be joining Mrs. Calloway for detention next week."

I froze. *Ugh.* He'd noticed me sneak in and it was impossible to hide my disappointment as I took my seat. I slipped my backpack off my shoulders and let it fall with a thud beside my chair.

"Now, if everyone will take their seat, I'll review one brief lesson before I hand out your problem set for the day."

Chase leaned in as I was reaching for my textbook. "Sorry, I really thought that would work."

I glanced over my shoulder and was met by his infectious grin.

"Cumulus was the best you could come up with?"

"I could have sworn that cloud looked like Mickey Mouse."

Connor grunted. "Gimme your man card, dude."

Chase's eyes met mine and we laughed just as Ashley's words echoed through my mind. She was right. Chase was one of the chosen people, but more than that, he was the last person I'd expected to be friends with upon my return to Blackwater. He and I had fought until the day I'd left town. It'd been a bitter war with two casualties and no spoils. I knew that, and yet his gravity still had a way of pulling me closer. I didn't have a single friend in Blackwater—not unless I counted Harvey—but out of everyone, every kid in my graduating class, Chase was the closest thing I had to an ally.

His mother would be disappointed.

CHAPTER THIRTY-FOUR

Chase

LILAH BOLTED FROM the classroom as soon as the bell rang. I walked to the front of the class to turn in my problem set and saw hers at the very bottom of the stack. Her name was written in scrolling cursive, so neat and perfect. I laid my paper down on top of it.

She knew I didn't have practice on Fridays, but she'd left without a second glance. I walked with Connor toward the parking lot, trying to work out her reasoning for leaving without me.

"So you're in love with her, right?"

His question caught me by surprise, but by the time I glanced over, my shock was masked by annoyance.

He held his hands up in innocence. "Jeez! I was kidding. You seriously can't take a joke these days."

I picked up the pace, weaving through students trying to make it to their cars. Unfortunately, he caught up easily.

"But seriously, you are, aren't you?"

The parking lot was packed with students, but I could see our group in the distance. Kimberly and Brian were talking with a few guys from the baseball team. I focused on them instead of looking at Connor, but that didn't stop him.

"I mean the googly eyes between you two are vomit-inducing."

I gripped the straps of my backpack and finally answered. "Let's say hypothetically that you're right, there's no point in dwelling on it."

His jaw dropped. "Why? Because she's a vampire?"

I had never wanted to punch Connor more in my life, but fortunately for him, we reached our group before I could turn and sock him in the face.

"Main-man-Matthews!" Brian called as I joined the circle of people milling around his car. Everyone always lingered on Fridays, trying to solidify weekend plans before parting ways. *Whose parents are out of town? Whose older brother can buy some alcohol?* It was the same questions week after week.

"Are you excited for your game this weekend?" Kimberly asked me with a big smile.

I thought back to when I'd briefly mentioned it to Lilah on the way to school; I didn't think she'd even been listening. "Yeah, but it's just a scrimmage, nothing serious."

Her smile never faltered. "I know, but I'll still be there with the Diamond Girls. It should be fun."

"Would you mind letting Lilah sit with you if she shows up?"

I asked the question before I realized how stupid it was. The odds of Lilah showing up for the game were slim at best. The chances of her sitting with Kimberly were astronomical.

CHAPTER THIRTY-FIVE

Lilah

SATURDAY AFTERNOON, I found myself walking into the baseball stadium at our high school wearing cutoff shorts and a Blackwater baseball shirt I'd found in the back of my closet. It was snug, but still fit well enough. I pulled my baseball cap lower and tucked a few strands of hair behind my ears.

"Lilah Calloway? Is that you hiding underneath that hat?"

I glanced up to see Mrs. Rochester behind the ticket booth. She was a friendly woman with a round build and a big smile. She would watch me when my dad brought me to the games when I was little. I hadn't seen her in a few years, but she looked nearly the same as she had back then.

"Hi Jan," I said with a small smile as I slid my five dollars across the counter for my ticket.

She pushed it right back toward me. "Oh please. Your

daddy would cut my hand off if I took your money."

"Oh, okay." I didn't feel like protesting, so I took the ticket she held out for me and pocketed my five dollars. "Thanks."

"Does he know you'll be here?" she asked with a kind smile.

I hadn't been to one of my dad's games in years. He had dragged me along when I was young, but once I was old enough to stay at home by myself, he let me decide what I wanted to do.

"I told him this morning," I said, recalling his reaction at the breakfast table. His eyebrows had practically met his hairline as I'd casually mentioned dropping by to watch him and the team.

"Well, I'm so happy you're here. I have to man the ticket booth until the second inning starts, but after that I'll come say hi to you in the stands," she promised as a young family walked up to purchase tickets.

As I walked away, I found myself hoping she actually meant what she'd said because I was fairly sure I'd be sitting by myself. Somehow I doubted Ashley and Trent were spending their Saturday afternoon rooting on the "Mighty Wolves" baseball team.

Truthfully, I didn't know why I was there. Chase had only mentioned the game in passing. It's not like he really expected me to show up. I told myself I was there for my dad or as a thank you to Chase for trying to get me out of detention; those reasons were easier to digest than the truth.

With a tug on the brim of my hat, I walked along the back of the bleachers, past the concession stand that sold Frito pies and hot dogs with enough chili sauce on them to send you into a cholesterol coma. The rich smells took me back to my childhood. My dad would give me five dollars before each game to spend at the concession stand. I remember feeling like a queen with ring pops as stand-in rubies. A bright neon poster confirmed that they were still four for a dollar. Say what you want about small town economies, but they sure are resistant to inflation.

It was a bright, warm day for February and I regretted not bringing a pair of glasses as I walked up the metal ramp to the bleachers. Texas didn't do spring very well. *Just like me.*

I'd barely breached the top of the ramp when I heard someone yell out for me.

"Lilah!"

I turned my head to follow the sound and found Kimberly sitting in the middle of a group of girls all wearing matching bright red, sparkly shirts with the words "Diamond Girls" printed across them. I hadn't realized that Kimberly would be at the game and I felt a mixture of relief and distress as I started to slowly walk toward her.

The other Diamond Girls watched me as I ascended the stairs toward them. As I reached the group, Kimberly stood and scooted out to greet me. Everyone shoved to the side, filling in her spot and opening up two new spots near the aisle.

"Hey!" she said, wrapping me in a hug that felt awkward and unexpected, but I hugged her back nonetheless. Kimberly was a hugger, and I was not. "Chase told me you might be here, but I wasn't sure if you'd make it."

I hadn't told him I'd be there. In another life—a more realistic life—I'd be lounging in bed, reading away my Saturday afternoon.

Before I could reply, Kimberly spoke up again. "Do you want to sit with us? We have room and it'd be fun to catch up." Her eyes twinkled with sincere kindness and I couldn't help but feel relief that she didn't hate me after I'd moved away without so much as a goodbye.

"Sure, yeah," I said as we both sat down and got situated on the cold metal bleachers. A few of the girls in the group waved and smiled at me. It seemed that as long as Kimberly approved of me sitting there, they weren't going to question it.

While we waited for the scrimmage to start, I studied their shirts up close and realized that each girl had a different player's last name and number on her back like a sports jersey. I shifted and tilted back to confirm my speculation. Kimberly's had "03-Matthews" on the back. She was Chase's "Diamond Girl".

Of course she was.

Why does that make my stomach hurt?

"So has it been hard living with Chase?" she asked with a gentle smile. Her blonde hair was hanging loose around her face, framing her cute features.

"Umm, it hasn't been too bad," I responded lamely. I wasn't sure where she and Chase stood and I wasn't about to divulge the fact that in the last two weeks he'd enjoyed walking in his towel back to his room after every one of his showers. It was slowly driving me insane.

"I can't imagine living with a boy," she said, almost wistfully. "Uh, I mean because they can be slobs," she recovered, scrunching her nose.

I shrugged. "Chase is good about cleaning up after himself."

"Ah, speaking of your roomie, there he is," she said, pointing out toward the field.

Chase was warming up on the pitcher's mound. He filled out the gray uniform so that the pants were tight around his thighs and legs, and the top stretched across his broad shoulders and trim waist. He rocked back on his left foot, planted his right against the white rubber strip, then coiled and uncoiled his body like a spring. His fastball made a crisp popping sound when it sunk into the catcher's mitt. Once, twice, three times he repeated the motions and I watched, completely enraptured by his confidence on the mound. His power and precision were amazing to behold, and I cursed myself for missing so many of his games.

"He's one of the best pitchers in the state. He might get drafted for the big leagues, but if not, he'll definitely play college ball," Kimberly said, pulling me out of my haze.

I turned to find her watching him with stars in her eyes, and I realized I'd looked just like her a moment before.

A few minutes later, I spotted my dad standing at the entrance of the dugout, leaning against the metal frame in his own version of the team's uniform. He spit out the shell of a sunflower seed and patted Chase's shoulder as he ran by. Whatever encouragement he'd offered, I couldn't hear it up in the stands.

"I'll be right back," I said to Kimberly as I hopped down the stairs toward my dad. My movement caught his eye and for a moment he let his "coach" face slip. He smiled wide and tugged his hat from his head. There was a layer of sweat collected on his tan forehead, but he wiped it off with his forearm.

Out of the corner of my eye, I could see a few women watching his every move; I wondered how many of them wished he'd finally settle back down. I shivered at the thought. I wasn't ready for another mom figure; I was still trying to get over the first one.

When he hit the railing, I bent down so he could reach up and give me a quick, sweaty hug.

"Hi Dad."

"Hi Lil. I'm glad you're here," he said with a warm smile.

"Wouldn't miss a scrimmage for the world," I joked as I stood back to my full height.

He laughed and shook his head. "Wait for me after the game. We'll go grab some pizza."

"Okay. Good luck," I said, starting to edge away from the railing just as Chase walked out of the dugout. His baseball cap was pulled low, blocking the light from his hazel eyes so that they were shadowed and dark. His smile slowly unpeeled as his gaze locked onto me. I could practically hear his thought: *You showed up.* We didn't say anything in that brief moment. The scrimmage was starting soon and he needed to stay focused, but that smile unraveled the strings around my heart, loosening their grip so that he could take hold even more. I shrugged and he smiled even wider, revealing his set of dimples before his teammates stepped out of the dugout to take the field.

He moved to stand in line and I stepped back to take my seat beside Kimberly. As each player from Blackwater was announced, his "Diamond Girl" stood and cheered with a sign that had the player's name on it. I tried to tell myself it didn't mean anything when Kimberly stood for Chase. She waved her sign wildly, causing a few pieces of glitter to fly off and land on my legs. I stared down at the gold specs as a dark, twisted feeling started to overtake my thoughts.

I'm a fraud.

Kimberly had been there watching and supporting Chase for the last two years. She made signs for him and wore his name on her shirt, and two weeks earlier I hadn't even been on speaking terms with him.

"Sorry about all this obnoxiousness," Kimberly

laughed, setting her poster down at her feet. "It's all tradition so we kind of just go with it."

I smiled tightly. "No, it's okay. I'm really glad Chase has you."

She stared at me for a moment, confused, but I turned toward the field before she could speak up.

The scrimmage began as expected, and I quickly learned the Diamond Girls were a sort of quasi-cheering section for the baseball team. They had chants for every moment of the game: between innings, when the other team went up to bat, and when their designated player made a play. Sometimes they'd chant while sitting down, but most of the time they all stood to do a little cheer and the crowd would join them.

The entire time, I fidgeted in my seat, feeling so horribly out of place that I wished I could have disappeared. I tried to concentrate on the game as best as I could. Chase was playing well, striking out player after player as the innings proceeded, but the pit in my stomach still grew, demanding to be felt.

"What are you doing after the game?" Kimberly asked after she and the Diamond Girls had wrapped up one particularly loud chant. I could feel her studying me, but I kept my eyes on the field.

"Oh, um, my dad said something about getting pizza."

I could see her smile out of the corner of my eyes. "Cool. I think we're going to go grab food with the team and then hang out somewhere after. Do you want me to text you wherever we end up?"

A normal, well-adjusted teenager would have said yes, but I didn't feel like hanging out with the Diamond Girls and the rest of the baseball team. I could picture myself sitting off to the side, feeling awkward and out of place. I appreciated her wanting to include me, but it just felt forced.

That's when I finally realized I didn't really fit in anywhere at my high school, not with the stoners, and not with the popular kids. My hiatus in Austin had succeeded in separating me from everyone. I was a complete loner.

"It's okay," I told her. "I woke up really early so I'll probably crash tonight."

Just as I finished explaining my lame excuse, my phone rang in my purse. I felt the vibration against my leg as I bent down to retrieve it. Ashley's name flashed across the screen and my gut clenched. She and I hadn't talked since the day before in the hallway.

I motioned to Kimberly that I was going to take the call and then walked down beneath the bleachers so I could talk without the noise from the crowd.

"Hey Ashley," I answered when I'd rounded the corner behind the restrooms.

"Wow, I'm surprised you even answered. I thought you only accepted phone calls from the chosen ones these days."

I assumed she was being icy because I hadn't called her the day before like I'd said I would.

"Whatever."

"What are you doing now? Want to come over to Trent's with me?"

My stomach rolled at the idea.

"I'm at a baseball game."

"Wait, wait. You're at the Blackwater baseball game right now? I thought you said you were going to lay low at your house this weekend?" Judgment dripped from every syllable. "Wow, I guess living with Chase really is changing you."

Something in her tone snapped a cord within me. I had let Ashley treat me like crap for the last two weeks and I'd brushed it off. I'd never really considered her a friend anyway, but she knew nothing about my life or why I made the decisions that I did. She knew nothing about my mom's death or my family's problems.

"I wanted to watch one of my dad's games before I graduate. You don't get to be rude to me because of it. Y'know, I thought I needed a friend to get through high school, but I'd rather be on my own than waste my time with people that are going to judge me for every little thing I do."

I exhaled a deep breath and realized I'd said much more than I had planned to.

"Wow, okay then, Miss Independent. Did that feel good?" she laughed.

I expected her to blow up on me or at the very least hang up, so her laughter surprised me.

"Yes." I smiled. "It did."

"I just wish you were coming," she began. "I know we don't have a ton in common, but this is a tiny town and options for friends are pretty limited."

I laughed at how blunt she was being. It was true that we were technically friends by default, but to say it out loud felt taboo.

"Let's hang out soon then. Maybe we can go see a movie," I answered, waving a white flag.

"Sounds good. I'll talk to you later."

I hung up the phone, feeling oddly lighter as I stepped back up toward the ramp. Clumps of people were filing down with their stadium chairs and trash in hand. The scrimmage must have ended while I was on the phone and I hadn't even realized. I fought against the flow of people to get back up to the bleachers. When I crested the top, I glanced over at the scoreboard. We'd won 14-4.

I turned toward the field. My dad was talking to the coach from the other school out on the pitcher's mound. The Blackwater team was lined up single file against the metal railing of the bleachers with the Diamond Girls lined up in front of them. Each Diamond Girl was in front of her designated player and when I saw Chase smiling up at Kimberly, I felt a punch to my gut. Kimberly bent down to talk to him over the noise of the stadium and I stood there for a moment, unsure of what to do.

Watching them together scraped at every one of my insecurities. They were quite the pair, the golden boy and the diamond girl. Their children would be royalty in this tiny town and I wanted to throw up.

When the players reached up to hand each of the Diamond Girls a red rose, I started walking backward down the ramp. I couldn't witness another second.

The moment they disappeared from my sight, the pressure in my chest lessened and I knew the right thing to do was to bow out of whatever unspoken competition was going on between Kimberly and me. Actually, to call it a competition was giving myself too much credit. I was broken; Kimberly was whole. I was selfish; Kimberly would give you the shirt off her back. She deserved to have Chase all to herself and by taking myself out of the competition, I could pretend that it didn't hurt as much as I walked away the loser.

I unlocked my phone and shot my dad a quick text.

Lilah: Let's do pizza at home instead.

CHAPTER THIRTY-SIX

Lilah

I LAID IN bed that night staring up at the shadows dancing across the surface of my ceiling. I'd already flipped onto every side of my body a half-dozen times, but sleep proved elusive. No position, pillow, or flock of sheep made it easier to stem the flow of thoughts from my mind.

When I'd gotten home after the game, I'd ordered pizza even though I wasn't hungry. My dad and I ate it while we watched a Friends rerun and at the very end of it, he glanced over to me.

"I'm really glad you came out today, Lilah. I know it meant a lot to Chase," he said.

I ignored the mention of Chase's name. "I came to see you, Dad. I'm proud of you, old man."

He laughed and shook his head. "Want to work in the garden tomorrow morning?"

I wondered if he could tell I had things weighing on my

mind. He would help me in the garden every now and then, but if he was asking, it meant he wanted to cheer me up.

Regardless, I nodded. "Yeah, I think the tomatoes are ready to be planted."

After staring at the first half of another *Friends* episode, I went up to my room and got ready for bed. It was early, but Chase wasn't home yet and I wanted to go to sleep and pretend I didn't know he was hanging out with Kimberly.

The idea of them together hurt.

I found myself pining for everything Kimberly had, and the notion of it shocked me. Two weeks before, I'd been living in another city, and now suddenly, I wanted to be Chase's best friend again. I wanted to be his dumb Diamond Girl, and I wanted him to hand me a rose at the end of the game and smile up at me like I was his world.

Admitting that only made the hurt sear into me a little deeper, so I rolled over and stared at my blank wall, trying to find another subject, any subject, to grasp on to. The next morning my dad and I would plant some heirloom tomatoes. I concentrated on the process: tilling the dirt, adding fertilizer and fresh mulch, picking a plot with full sunlight and well-drained soil, digging a hole wide enough for the plant to fit into without it being too deep, adding a cage so the plant could hold its own weight...

A door opened in the hallway. I looked up and held my breath trying to pinpoint which door had opened: my dad's or Chase's. When I heard the soft rumble of game footage, I knew Chase still wasn't home.

I flipped onto my back and blew out a puff of air. My hands clenched the sheets and I willed my mind to turn off so I could get seven hours of thoughtless sleep. I blinked, then squeezed my eyes shut, then arched my neck to readjust my head on my pillow, and then finally I sat up to beat my lumpy pillow into submission.

When I'd had enough, I decided to find some NyQuil in my bathroom and see if that would knock me out.

It took a moment to adjust to the bright light when I flipped the switch on in the bathroom, but when I did, the first thing I saw was my mother's eyes staring back at me in the mirror.

Drugs had changed her, physically and emotionally. They'd aged her face, marring it with deep-set wrinkles. They'd yellowed her teeth and left the stench of death in her breath. They'd thinned her hair and tattered her fingernails. Her cheekbones had hollowed, her eyes sunk behind dark circles, but there was no changing that eye color. Her pale green eyes were in her genome, the same way they were in mine.

I leaned forward and stared into the mirror without blinking. I studied the coloring in my eyes, trying to see beneath their surface. They looked like two cut emeralds, rimmed with a deep, dark green.

I studied one and then the other, trying to find subtle traces of her, which is probably why I didn't notice Chase until he was standing right behind me. He was a blur of features and then I shifted my gaze and met his eyes in the mirror. The light hazel was a refreshing change.

"I won't turn into my mom," I said.

"I know," he nodded.

"I won't become what she was," I said, emphasizing my point.

"Then don't," he said, swaying gently from side to side, slowly enough that I had to tilt my head to confirm that the movement was actually happening.

"Are you drunk?" I said, spinning away from his reflection to take in the real flesh and blood.

"I was on the mound," he began, ignoring my question. "I struck out the last batter and when I looked up in the stands, you weren't there. Why weren't you there?" His eyebrows were tugged together, knit down the center of his forehead in frustration.

"I was there. I was there the whole time, but Ashley called and I couldn't ignore her," I explained. "By the time I came back, the game was over."

My words didn't seem to mean anything as his demeanor stayed the same. "I wanted you to be there waiting for me," he said.

"Kimberly was waiting for you." The words were out before I'd even formed them in my mind.

"Lilah," he warned with a harsh tone.

"What? I wasn't going to stand behind her in line to talk to you. I'm not a competitive person, and I know when it's time to bow out." I was being immature, and still, I couldn't rise above it. I couldn't be the person Chase needed me to be.

"I kissed her tonight," he said, stepping forward so that I had to take a step back. "Kimberly."

I took another step back and the back of my thighs hit the cold sink; I had nowhere else to go.

"Is that what you want to hear?" he asked. "That I kissed her because I was drunk and pissed at you?"

"Chase, stop."

"No," he said, caging my body against the sink with his arms as he bent lower. His face was level with mine and I could smell the beer on his breath. I hated that he still looked so painfully handsome. I didn't want to think he was handsome; I wanted to go back to before, when no one could hurt me and I kept everyone at arm's length. Maybe I hadn't been happy, but at least I was safe, content, constant.

"I'm glad you kissed her," I lied through my teeth.

"No you aren't," he argued.

I squeezed my eyes closed and turned my head so that I wouldn't be tempted to lean forward and close the gap between our lips.

"I won't fight over you."

"Maybe I want you to fight *for* me," he said, skimming his cheek against mine.

I pinched my eyes closed. "You're drunk. You won't remember any of this in the morning."

"You know what?" He leaned forward and his breath hit my earlobe. "She'll never be you, Lilah."

I absorbed his words in two slow breaths.

"You need sleep," I offered with a gentle tone.

"You don't know what I need," he argued with a fury building behind his hazel eyes. He hauled his body against mine and his chest hit me with enough force to knock the wind out of me, but when his lips met mine—that's when he stole my breath.

My fingers wound through his hair, trying to keep him at a safe distance, but his hands gripped my waist, lifting me back up onto the bathroom sink. I wound my legs around his hips and lost sight of everything beyond him. In a black and white world, Chase and I would never end up together—our mothers had ensured that—but in that small bathroom, under the harsh fluorescent lights, we dragged each other deeper into the gray—the messy, guilt-ridden space that sat between right and wrong.

He broke the kiss and I propped my hands on the bathroom sink, trying hard to stay upright on my own.

"*That's* what I need," he said before storming out of the bathroom and leaving me swaying back and forth on the sink, searching for the heart he'd just ripped from my chest.

I flipped the bathroom light and the room went dark. I'd never asked him to take me to the gray. I was perfectly happy living in the black.

CHAPTER THIRTY-SEVEN

Chase

I SLAMMED MY bedroom door behind me and flipped on the light. Harvey had been asleep on my bed, and the noise from the door jarred him awake. My back rested against the cold wood as I watched Harvey watching me. His eyes were wide as he waited for my next move, but I didn't have a next move.

I hated how stubbornly I loved Lilah. She could tear me in two and I'd still come back. A dark part of me wanted to hate her. It'd be so much easier if I thought she was as evil as she thought she was, but I knew the secret she tried so hard to hide: she was scared shitless, scared of letting anything happen between us, scared of looking past everyone's flaws to get to the real meat of life.

I'd thought she'd left the baseball game early. I'd concentrated hard on the game, knowing she was up in the stands watching me. When the game had ended and I'd looked up to find her seat empty, it had hurt more than I cared to admit. I'd gone through the motions of postgame traditions. We'd passed out roses to the Diamond Girls and then Connor had dragged me to his house for a party. I hadn't wanted to go; I'd wanted to hunt Lilah down and force her to explain why she couldn't be there for me even once.

After four beers at Connor's house, I'd told myself Kimberly was who I belonged with. She was pretty and simple—so fucking simple it made no sense why I wasn't into her. She never let me down, she never moved away, she never pretended not to love me.

I never should have kissed her.

"I don't like you any more," Kimberly laughed as I *stepped away. "And you definitely don't like me either."*

I cringed.

She shrugged. "I think every girl at our high school has had a crush on you at least once, but I think I'm finally over you. Brian and I have been hanging out lately and he asked me to go out on a date with him next weekend."

I couldn't believe Brian had actually worked up the courage to ask her out.

"And...obviously you're so in love with Lilah you can't even see straight."

I wiped my hand down my face. "Yeah, well I'm not sure that will ever be reciprocated."

She laughed. "Are you kidding? Did you not hear what I just said? Every girl has had a crush on you, and even Lilah Calloway isn't immune to your charms. She was staring at you the whole time. If her dad wasn't the coach, I would've assumed she had never seen a game of baseball before."

I narrowed my eyes, trying to figure out if Kimberly was telling the truth. She had nothing to gain from lying, so I shrugged and changed the subject.

"Don't tell Brian about that kiss. I'm drunk."

She laughed. "Consider it closure."

Harvey slid off the bed to sniff around my heels. I leaned down to pet him, trying to work out if I needed to go on a late night run. I had too much energy to sleep, but I knew I'd throw up as soon as my feet hit the pavement. Instead, I reached under my bed for my tools and my box of cameras. I dropped the box onto my desk and rifled through it until I found the slim brown case at the very bottom. Inside, there was a vintage Leica M3 I'd found online a few months earlier. It was from 1952 and had been almost beyond repair when it'd first arrived. I'd been working on it slowly, trying to prolong the process so that I wouldn't finish and then have to sell it. It was a rare find, worth too much to keep, but now I had a better idea for it.

CHAPTER THIRTY-EIGHT

Lilah

AFTER THE MOST restless night of sleep I'd ever had, I lay in bed listening to the sounds of our aging house and trying to ignore the sinking feeling in my gut. It was a physical sign of my stress and I knew it wouldn't go away until I straightened out the creases of my life. Chase was the first item on that list.

How could he look at me every day when I had the same green eyes as my mother? I was a part of her no matter how hard I tried to pretend I wasn't. He could pull me into the gray, we could pretend that we were good and happy there, but in the end, we'd always be living with ghosts.

I pushed my blankets off me and crawled out of bed. The house stayed quiet as I threw on a t-shirt and the same pair of tattered jeans I'd always worn when I gardened. There were holes in the knees from leaning down to dig in the dirt, but they fit me well and I couldn't bear the thought of replacing them.

Once my gardening gloves were shoved into my back pocket, I opened my door and stepped out into the hallway. Chase's door was closed, and the gap between the door and the carpet was dark; he was still asleep. I stepped past his room and headed down the stairs in search of a banana and some water. I'd take a break later to have a real breakfast; I was anxious to get started.

It was early in the season, but I was growing my plants from seeds and in Texas it's better to get started early or the crops have to wrestle with summer heat. As I stepped out onto the porch, I took a deep breath and tried to ignore the lingering knot in my stomach.

With sharp concentration, I studied my plots and chewed bites of banana. The backyard wasn't much to look at yet, but in a few months, each of the raised plots would be brimming over with life. My dad had repaired them and now the only thing left to do was fill them up with soil and mulch.

I finished off my banana, set the peel aside, and then stepped out onto the grass.

The small shed near the fence was designated for our lawn mower and gardening equipment. I pulled open the wooden door and inhaled the quintessential earthy must that lingers around bagged mulch. My dad had taken the time to stock it full of supplies for the year, saving me the trip into town. I shot him a mental thank you and then started counting out the bags. I was halfway done when the house's screen door creaked open.

When I spun around, I found my dad with a cup of coffee and a warm smile. He had on a Henley t-shirt and his gardening jeans, just like I did, except his looked even more worse for wear.

"I swear you start earlier every year," he teased, taking a sip of coffee that I knew from experience was black as tar. I'd once stolen a sip of it as a kid and spit it out across the kitchen table. The black splatter had stained the wood before anyone had gotten around to cleaning it.

"I just like to start when there's still a chill in the air. It'll get up into the high 80s later today."

He nodded and took another long sip from his mug.

"Vegetables or fruits first?" he asked.

"Fruits. They'll be easier. I'm only doing watermelon and strawberries in the beds this year."

"Thought you wanted to do that raspberry plant?" he asked.

My mom and I had tried and failed to grow a raspberry vine year after year.

"I do, but I've got to plant it along the fence so the vines have something to hang on to," I explained.

He set his coffee on the porch with a hollow thunk. "They seem like they'll be high maintenance."

Just like her.

"I think I'll be able to get them to grow," I said just as the screen door creaked opened again.

Like the sun coming out from behind a cloud, Chase stepped onto the back porch wearing a simple white t-shirt and faded blue jeans. He was barefoot and his hair was tousled from sleep. He let loose a yawn just as the screen door hit the wood frame behind him.

"Morning Chase. Hope we didn't wake you," my dad said.

He shook his head and tried in vain to tame his hair before giving up altogether. "Nah. I couldn't sleep so I figured I'd come down and help." He paused and looked past my dad, his hazel eyes finding me standing in the doorway of the shed. "If that's okay..."

My dad turned to look at me with a funny expression and I knew if I said no, he would probably chastise me for being rude.

I shrugged and turned back to the shed. "The more the merrier."

My dad finished off his coffee, Chase stepped off the porch, and then we all got busy forming an assembly line. My dad handed off the bags of mulch to Chase, Chase carried them to the beds, and I tore into them with a pair of gardening scissors. Each bed needed a couple bags, so eventually we were all working together, tearing open the plastic and pouring the bags out into even piles.

Chase knelt down at the bed across from me as my fingers dug into the fresh dirt. I tried not to glance up, but I did anyway. The morning light caught his blond hair in a way that made it hard to ignore. His face was evenly tanned from his baseball game the day before, and when he glanced up and caught me staring, I shifted my gaze back down as quickly as possible.

"I saw that banana peel on the porch. What's that for?" Chase asked with no trace of arrogance in his tone; maybe he hadn't noticed me watching him.

"I'm going to use it for my raspberries."

He tilted his head toward me and cocked his brows. "For mulch?"

I nodded.

A few moments later he went back into the house and then came back out with a banana of his own. In true teenage-boy fashion, he ate it in three bites and then met my eye as he let the peel fall on top of mine.

"For the raspberries," he said with his right hand over

his heart and a smile that was too charming for his own good.

I chuckled under my breath and shook my head.

"Are you ready for the seeds yet, Lilah?" my dad asked from inside the shed.

I glanced around to the eight beds filled with new, rich soil. "Yup. Let's do the watermelons first."

Three hours later, most of the beds were full of seeds, patted down, and watered. The seeds would hopefully sprout within a week or two and we'd know if we needed to plant more or not. I sat back on my heels and admired our hard work.

"I'm starving. Are you guys hungry?" my dad asked as he stood and dusted himself off.

"Yes!" Chase and I bellowed at the same time. I hadn't ever stopped to eat anything besides that banana and my stomach was grumbling in protest.

"All right. I'll run into town and grab some hamburgers."

We rattled off specifications—no pickles for me, extra cheese for Chase—and then he set off for food. I was practically salivating at the thought of a hamburger, but I knew it would take my dad at least twenty minutes to get there and back, so I tried to keep busy continuing to plant seeds.

"Let's take a break," Chase said, leaning back on his heels with a sigh.

I looked up at him and then laughed. There was dirt streaked across his cheek and his hair was a wild mess, even more so than when he'd first woken up.

"What? Is something funny?" he asked with a wicked gleam in his eye.

I pointed toward his cheek. "I think you've got a little

something on your face."

He swiped aimlessly at his mouth, chin, and forehead. I couldn't tell if he was intentionally missing the spot or not, but either way I pushed off the ground and rounded the flowerbed. When I was crouched down in front of him, I reached up with my thumb and wiped his cheek. The dirt hardly budged.

"Did you get it?" he asked, hopeful.

I chuckled and licked my thumb to see if it would help. The dirt was caked on really well.

He flinched when I brought my thumb back to his face. "Oh, gross. Now you're just wiping your spit on me."

"No! I swear half your cheek is covered in dirt," I laughed.

Before I could even react, he reached into the bed and wiped some dirt across my cheek.

"Chase!"

He shrugged. "There. Now we're even."

Over my dead body.

I reached for a handful of dirt and took aim directly at him.

"Wait!" he yelled, holding up his hands in defense. "You don't want to do that!"

My eyebrow arched on its own accord. "Oh, I think I do." The dirt he'd rubbed onto my cheek was cold and damp from the garden hose. It slipped down my face like sludge and then a small splatter hit the top of my shoulder. I didn't wait another second; I threw the wad of dirt directly at him and it landed square in the center of his white T-shirt.

"Lilah!" he bellowed as he lunged forward and caught my wrists in his hands. I instinctively tried to get away but I couldn't move while he held me. I wiggled around and fell onto my back. He leaned over me with a confident smile, silhouetted by the sun behind him.

"Let me go, Chase."

"I don't think that would be fair. You just slung a dirt clod at an unarmed man." His smirk didn't budge and the longer it was present, the harder it was to convince my heart to slow its wild beat.

"You did it to me first," I pointed out.

He nodded and his head fell an inch closer to mine. My eyes traveled to his lips on instinct.

"So maybe we should get even once and for all?" he asked. My breath caught in my throat and I knew he could hear the blood rioting in my body.

"About last night..." I began, feeling the blush creep up my cheeks as I thought about our kiss. I couldn't even look at his lips without remembering the feel of them on my mine.

"What about last night?" he dared, keeping his hazel eyes pinned on me.

"Um." I couldn't think with him so close. His knee was wedged between my legs and his grip was tight around my wrists. The scent of his body wash was enough to confuse my logic. "We shouldn't do it again."

"Do what?" he challenged.

"Kiss."

"So you don't want me to lean down and kiss you right now?" he asked with an amused grin.

I pressed my lips together as if I feared he would act on his words, and then I shook my head no.

"I'm sorry, I didn't hear that."

"I—"

My dad's truck rumbled into the driveway, cutting our moment short and saving me from a stuttered reply. I listened to his engine cut off and then the truck door slammed closed. Chase let go of my wrists and pushed off the ground to stand. He'd been blocking the sun before and when he moved away, I had to squeeze my eyes shut from the blinding glare.

It was too bright.

CHAPTER THIRTY-NINE

Lilah

MY SCHOOL'S WINDOWS didn't get cleaned as regularly as they should have. It was nearly impossible to see past the dirt and dust, but if I tried hard enough, I could see the perimeter fence and the fields that lay beyond. I focused there at the start of my detention, trying to count the rows of dirt to keep my brain occupied. I didn't want to think of Chase or my mom. The two of them already had ownership of my mind at night when there was nothing to distract me. They'd duel it out in the darkness of my room, tugging me back and forth like I was the leading lady in some sort of twisted love triangle.

Every step I took toward Chase, every time I let my guard down even an inch, I could feel my mother's ghost twist around me, rooting me to the ground like a poisonous vine. I resented her for it, the way she could claw her way back from the dead. I'd foolishly assumed that death would finally take her away from me.

A student slipped into the spare seat in front of me, slinging his backpack so that it slammed into the stack of textbooks on my desk. Half of them went sliding off onto the ground and the chaos of the moment pulled me out of my staring contest with the cornfields.

"Oh, shit. Sorry," he said, reaching down to grab the fallen books.

He pushed them back onto my desk and I waved off his apology, trying to decide if I had the willpower to open any of the books that were now restacked haphazardly on my desk. I was already ahead in all of my classes, but I wouldn't survive an hour in detention without some sort of distraction.

Mrs. Nicholson—the poor teacher who'd been lucky enough to land detention duty—instructed everyone to have a seat and get comfortable. I glanced up at the large black clock that hung above the whiteboard at the front of the class. According to the plodding hands of the clock, I had fifty-nine minutes until freedom. With a sigh, I flipped open my literature textbook and turned to a chapter we weren't due to cover for a few weeks.

There was a knock on the classroom door, but I kept my focus on my textbook, trying to reread a sentence until it stuck.

"Mr. Matthews, what can I do for you?" Mrs. Nicholson asked.

My gaze flew up to see Chase standing in the doorway wearing a confident smile, a Blackwater High School sweatshirt, and faded jeans.

"I need to grab Lilah Calloway," he said, holding up a slip of paper. "She has a meeting with the college counselor."

I glanced down at my book to hide my smile. Chase Matthews was lying to a teacher.

Mrs. Nicholson turned to the room. "Is there a Lilah Calloway in here?"

I raised my hand gently.

She nodded and pointed toward the door.

"Right. Hurry out so we don't have further interruptions."

I shoved my books into my backpack, zipped it up, and made my way to the door. A few of the students whistled low under their breath as I passed. Rumors about Chase and me had been circulating since the stone ages, but since I'd moved back, they'd started up again with a vengeance. I purposely looked past Chase as I walked out of the door, and it wasn't until we were out in the hallway that I stopped and eyed him with a skeptical smile.

"Show me what's on that piece of paper," I said, holding out my hand.

He'd written a hall pass in chicken-scratch that wouldn't have passed the inspection of a ten-year-old.

"Lilah Calloway to see Mrs. Hill for a 4:00 PM appointment," I read aloud.

I glanced back up to Chase. His hazel eyes watched me with curiosity and I was torn between wanting to thank him and wanting to run far, far away.

"You know if she'd actually looked at this piece of paper, she'd have realized that this wasn't on school stationery. Also, that's not the counselor's name."

"What?" he laughed and swiped the note back to reread it. "I thought her name was Mrs. Hill."

"It's Mrs. Heaney."

His brows shot up. "Huh. I've talked to her like five

165

times and I never knew."

I laughed. "Why'd you actually pull me out of detention?"

"I have a taste for adventure," he said, waggling his eyebrows seductively. My stomach dipped in anticipation. "Let's go before someone sees us out here."

I had no clue where he was leading me, but I followed him blindly. Chase had found a loophole to my evasiveness: trust him, or go back to detention.

"If someone stops us, tell them you're going to see your dad because you don't feel well," he explained.

No one was going to stop us. The final bell had only rung fifteen minutes earlier and students were still lingering in the hallways. Chase held the back door open for me and I slipped on my sunglasses. The sun was bright for late February and I knew my flowerbeds back home were appreciating the warmth.

I followed him around the school, straight past the parking lot. I knew if I looked, I'd find people watching us, so I kept my head forward and trudged on. His beat up truck was parked outside of the perimeter fence. He rounded the front and opened my door for me, ushering me inside with a wave of his arm.

"Check the seat before you sit," he warned.

I glanced down to find a small worn camera case sitting on the passenger side of the bench seat. I reached for it, feeling the soft brown leather beneath my fingertips.

"Is this yours?"

"It was, but now it belongs to you."

I narrowed my eyes, twisting the case around my hands. "What do you mean?"

"What good is a sleuth without a camera?"

I unclipped the flap of the case and pulled out the

vintage camera, holding it in my hand like a baby bird.

"It's a vintage 1952 Leica M3," he declared.

I glanced back to see him eyeing the camera in my hands with a proud smile stretched across his lips. "Does it work?"

He laughed. "No, Lilah. I gave you a broken camera."

I rolled my eyes. "It just looks so old."

"I promise it's good as new, and it even has a serial number that's over 1,000,000. Collectors love those because it means it was built near the end of this model's production, so the factory workers were at the top of their game," he explained. "Now hop in and I'll teach you how to use it."

I gripped the camera and stepped toward the truck before the weight of reality slammed down around me.

I can't leave with Chase.

It was so easy to pretend things were normal, that we were normal, but in reality, we were a thousand miles from it. I eased away from the truck, clutched the camera in my hand, and shook my head. Chase frowned as I thanked him for getting me out of detention and he stood there dumbfounded as I turned and walked away.

Every step I took away from him made it easier to clear my head.

It was easy to gravitate toward Chase. He had the charm and the smile and the heart. He promised happiness and I'd almost let myself believe him, but I knew better.

My mother had ruined Hannah; I refused to ruin Chase.

• • •

Chase

To me, Lilah meant late nights sneakin' out, moonlit hair, and sparklers in July. She'd been the brightest part of my childhood and now she was evading me at all costs. She thought she was doing me a favor by giving me space, she thought my hatred for her mom extended to her as well. I was sure she'd worked out some convoluted explanation in her mind, but the truth was I loved Lilah even as she walked away from me that day.

I would always love Lilah.

CHAPTER FORTY

Chase

IT'D BEEN A month since I had heard from my dad. I worked at the shop every Sunday and left him dozens of voicemails, but he never called me back.

Late Thursday night, I paced back and forth in my room trying to get ahold of him. My first two calls had already gone to voicemail, but I resolved to try one last time.

When the call connected, I nearly dropped the phone.

"Dad?"

"Chase. Hey. Can you hear me?"

"Yeah. Is this a good time to talk?" I asked.

"Oh, sure…sure. How are you, bud?"

There was an edge to his voice, a slight slur, and I knew without a doubt that he'd been drinking.

"I'm good," I offered, moving around my bedroom so that Harvey's gaze followed my trail. "How have things been over there?"

He coughed and I waited for him to answer me. When he didn't, I trudged on.

"I could come over for dinner or something soon."

"Oh, no no. It's not a good time for that. I'm real behind at the shop. Might have to close it up, with the economy and everything."

I pinched my eyes closed. I couldn't believe him.

"What are you going to do for money then?" I asked. An eighteen-year-old kid should never have to ask his father that question.

"Chase, don't start with that," he grumbled. "I've got everything figured out and I don't need you breathing down my neck. You just worry about baseball. You doin' good? How are you playing this season?"

It was almost worse that he knew the season was happening. He had never missed a single game before my mom died; he'd only managed to attend one or two after her death.

"It's been a good season, Dad. Coach Calloway thinks we have a chance of going to state if we keep playing like we are."

The unmistakable sound of glass shattering in the background served as the period to my sentence.

"Oh shoot. Dammit. Chase, I gotta go," he said just before the line went dead. I pulled the phone away from my face and looked down at it in disbelief. The call was over. Just like that, my dad was gone again. My finger hovered over his name as I battled with the urge to call him back, but before I could hit send, a small knock sounded at my door.

"Chase?" Lilah called from the other side of the door.

"Hey, yeah. I'm in here," I called out.

The thin door popped open and Lilah's face peeked

through. "Um, would it be okay if I took Harvey on a walk? Just a short one around the block?"

Harvey's head jerked up at the sound of his favorite four-letter word and I knew there was no point in resisting. He'd already hopped off the bed and joined Lilah by the door before I'd even worked out my answer. Besides, he needed the exercise, especially if I was going to be away at the shop all night.

I nodded and grabbed my truck keys off my desk. "Yeah, go ahead. I'm going to head up to my dad's shop."

Lilah hesitated in the doorway and when I glanced up at her, she was frowning down at Harvey.

"What?"

Her bright eyes met mine. "Isn't it kind of late for that?"

"Isn't it kind of late for a walk?"

"I just want to clear my head," she explained, standing her ground.

It was settled then. I tightened my grip around my keys and moved past her.

If I drove quick, I could finish up four or five repair jobs before I crashed. My dad needed a hell of a lot more help, but it was better than sitting and doing nothing. I was halfway down the stairs, lost in the stress of the shop, when Lilah called out after me.

"Chase."

I turned back and caught sight of her at the top of the stairs, toying with the end of her long-sleeved shirt.

"Yeah?"

She hesitated and then nodded toward the front door.

"I'll leave the light on for you."

CHAPTER FORTY-ONE

Lilah

ON FRIDAY AFTERNOON, I went out back to inspect my garden, relieved to find tiny, fragile plants waiting for me. They'd sprouted up over night, dozens of nearly identical twins that would grow into a variety of plants over the next few weeks. I bent down in front of the first flowerbed and ran my finger across the new leaves. They were velvety soft and in desperate need of water. I turned on the hose and dragged it over to the first bed.

"Lilah."

An unfamiliar voice carried over the grass and I turned to find Trent standing on the back porch, holding on to the wooden post with a nervous smile. I hadn't talked to him in weeks and suddenly, there he was in his leather jacket and faded black jeans. His messy hair and Doc Martens completed his misunderstood-teen look.

I motioned for him to give me a minute and finished

watering the beds. When the soil was damp and dark brown, I turned off the hose and headed for the porch. I slipped out of my gardening shoes and left them on the porch to dry. Trent stood, watching me.

"What are you doing here?" I asked, eyeing the path he'd taken around the house.

He brushed his hand through his hair and shrugged. "I was driving around town, didn't feel like going home. I figured I'd stop by and see if you were around."

I hadn't talked to Trent since I'd seen him outside my mom's apartment complex.

"I was just watering my garden," I said, trying to navigate the awkward situation. "Did you need something or...do you want to come in?"

He tucked his arms across his chest. "You don't have to invite me in or anything. I should have asked before coming over."

I recognized desperation in Trent's eyes. I knew what it was like to not want to go home. I didn't know his story, but if he needed a place to hang out for the afternoon, I wasn't going to kick him out.

"C'mon, I need a snack anyway."

He smiled as I propped the screen door open for him.

"I don't think I've ever been inside your house," he admitted, turning in a circle and taking in the kitchen. There were two pictures hanging on the wall, both equally ancient. My family—including my mom—smiled up at the camera in one photo, and directly next to it there was a photo of the Matthews family with a baby-faced Chase.

"What's with the photo of Chase Matthews in your kitchen? Are you guys related?" he asked, tapping his finger on the glass.

I didn't look at the photo. "Our moms were best friends

growing up, so our families were really close."

He studied the photo for another moment before shrugging. I told him to take a seat at the table as I rooted through our pantry. It'd been a week or two since anyone had gone to the grocery store, but there were still some chips left. I tossed the bag onto the table and grabbed an apple from the fruit bowl on the counter.

Trent watched me take a bite of apple and then he tore into the bag of chips.

"Are you the only one home?" he asked.

The house was eerily quiet with Chase and my dad gone. Normally I could count on my dad's game footage humming through the house.

"Yeah, not sure where the guys are." I purposely skipped over saying Chase's name because I knew Trent was itching to talk about him.

"I still don't get why he's living here," he said.

I rolled my eyes. Trent and I weren't dating—in fact we were hardly even friends—and yet he still felt like he had some sort of claim over me.

Before I could cut off all further discussion of him, the front door creaked open and sunlight streamed in with Chase. His backpack hit the floor near the door and I squeezed my eyes shut, praying he'd skip the kitchen and head straight upstairs.

"Lilah?"

I opened my eyes and glanced over to look at him. His jaw tightened as he registered Trent's presence, but he didn't say a word as he stepped into the kitchen.

"No soccer practice today?" Trent asked with a bitter edge to his words.

Chase opened the refrigerator and bent down to inspect its contents. "Baseball, and it just finished."

Trent grunted and I scooted my chair back, preparing for the inevitable showdown.

"I think it's probably time for you to go," I said, offering Trent a weak smile.

He laughed and scraped his chair away from the table.

"Sorry," I added lamely.

He shook his head. "Don't be sorry. I get it. The golden boy is home so you're done with me for now."

• • •

Chase

"Is there something you want to say to me, Trent?" I called across the room.

Lilah and Trent twisted around to stare at me and I knew I should have kept my mouth shut. Trent was leaving. That's what I wanted.

Trent narrowed his eyes on me, but Lilah was quicker. She reached behind him and opened the front door to usher him out before I could dig myself in any deeper.

"Who the fuck does he think he is?" Trent asked as Lilah pushed him through the door.

"Just leave it. It's not worth it," she said, pushing harder against his chest. "I'll see you around school or something."

Once he was clear of the door, she slammed it closed and spun around to stare at me.

"Was that necessary? Don't start acting like you own the place. He needed a place to hang out for a few hours— you of all people should understand that."

We were standing across the living room from each other. My eyes were on her, but her gaze was on the front door. Her fists were clenched and her jaw ticked back and forth. I wasn't afraid of her anger; I was afraid of her silence. I didn't want her to shrivel back into her shell and pretend like we didn't have two years of pent up anger we needed to hash out.

For two seconds I thought she was going to fight with me, to yell at me about what was *really* bothering her, and then she shook her head and made for the stairs.

I moved quicker and blocked her path.

"Let me by," she insisted.

"No."

She couldn't get around me with my arms crossed and when she tried, I moved to block her path. I'd waited two years to talk to her about our past and I was sick of skating around it. I always swept it under the rug, too scared to ruin her mood, but she was already pissed, so it was now or never.

She shifted her weight onto her right leg, crossed her arms, and stared at the wall behind my head.

So goddamn stubborn.

"Yell at me. Talk to me," I said with a gentle tone, trying to coax her into being honest. "You're not mad about Trent. I know you're not mad about that."

"Get. Out. Of. My. Way," she spoke, enunciating each word.

"Do something, Lilah!" I argued.

Her hand shot out too fast for me to realize what she was doing. I felt a sharp sting on my cheek and then I reached up to touch it as her eyes grew as wide as saucers.

"I'm sorry. Please just let me by," she said with a quivering lip. "I don't want to fight about it right now."

The explosion was over before it even began. She was recoiling into herself and taking the truth with her. I couldn't let that happen.

"No more bullshit, Lilah."

She tried to get by me again, and when I blocked her path, she threw her hands in the air, defeated but angry.

"What do you want from me?!" she cried, her voice growing louder. "GIVE IT UP, CHASE!"

"I want you to talk to me! *Really* talk to me. We went through the same thing! No one will understand how you feel more than I do!"

Her eyes turned into two little slits and she balled her hands into tight fists. She was angrier than I'd ever seen her and instead of caving like she wanted me to, I held my ground.

"I don't want to talk about the past Chase!" Her words were venom ejected through clenched teeth. "I NEVER WANT TO TALK ABOUT IT!"

I blinked, then blinked again.

Devastation hung in the air between us, waiting for an answer.

I fisted my hands and shook my head. "No. You can't shut me out forever, Lilah. That night wasn't your fault."

"STOP!"

"You're not the victim here and neither am I!"

She clenched her hands even tighter. "Don't you get it?! We all became her victims! We still are!"

CHAPTER FORTY-TWO

August 2013
Blackwater, Texas

THE CIGARETTE SMOKE swirled through the air, curling in on itself and then dissipating in front of the apartment window. Elaine held her cigarette to her chapped lips and took another long drag, letting her eyelids flutter at the rush of nicotine. She was only halfway done, but she felt in her pocket for the nearly empty pack, finding relief in its presence.

Her hand shook as she flipped open the lid and pulled out another cigarette, tapping it against the window in beat with her heart. She'd stood there all day, watching and waiting. Her legs were tired and her stomach had long ago given up on food, but her mind's discomfort was far greater than her body's. The parking lot in front of her apartment was dark—always dark thanks to the street lamp that had burned out the year before.

Even without the light, she could see the black Camaro as it turned into the parking lot. There was no need to turn to the clock on her kitchen wall; she knew they were right on time. Donny was punctual.

The four men slid out of the dark car: Donny and his crew. Two of them were new, guys she'd never had the pleasure of seeing before. Their jeans were torn and their beards were long and unkempt. The one trailing the group pulled a little bag from his back pocket, measured out a hit with his pinkie fingernail, and snorted it, shaking his head as the cocaine took effect.

Donny's partner, Carl, led the group. Carl was a skinny, sharp-featured man that Elaine had always assumed was a demon come to life. Dark, spiraling tattoos slithered up the sides of his neck, overtaking his face completely. The only features left intact were his dark eyes, staring straight at her through the thin window. She whipped the curtain closed and turned around, assessing the situation. None of them carried weapons; they concealed them. She knew from experience Donny always had a switchblade in his right pocket. The blade was dull and stained from use, and she prayed he wouldn't use it when he killed her.

"Elaine, open the fucking door," Donny said as his fist hammered on the thin particleboard.

She inhaled the longest drag of her life, and then pressed the lit end of the cigarette hard into her forearm. The sharp pain brought her eyes into focus, and the flood of adrenaline made her feel strong, if only for this moment.

This moment had been coming for months, years even. Addiction came with a price, and she'd always known the devil would eventually show up to collect his due. Even so, as she unlocked the deadbolt and turned the handle, she suddenly had the urge to run. She wanted to turn back for the window, slide it open, and slip out into the night like she'd done as a little girl.

She wasn't ready to die.

She wasn't ready to leave Lilah.

She thought of her daughter as Donny kicked open the door with so much force it cracked the drywall behind it. Elaine jumped back out of the way and Donny stepped inside, bringing with him the smell of liquor and rot.

Donny's thin lips twisted into a grin. "Nice to see you, Elaine."

She took another step back as the four men walked into her apartment, claiming the space as their own. She avoided eye contact, staring instead at their shoes. Black, heavy boots stained her carpet, leaving trails of dirt and sludge that she'd never have to scrub away; it'd be a problem for the tenant that came after her.

The new guys trailed through her house, turning over her living room and tossing her couch cushions onto the ground. They took knives to the pillows, ripping open the material to get to the stuffing. They were looking for money, but they wouldn't find any.

Carl and Donny stepped into her kitchen and Donny pushed the contents of her kitchen table onto the ground, sweeping her belongings away so easily that she had to squeeze her eyes closed as her life scattered across the linoleum floor.

He spun a chair around and took a seat with his legs hanging over each side. "Y'know, I'm sad to see it end this way Elaine. I was really pulling for you. There aren't many whores like you in this shitty town. You know that?"

Elaine turned to him, but she couldn't meet his eye. She

focused on the scar that stretched down his face, specifically at the point where it ended halfway into his lip. Someone had nearly sliced him in two when he was younger and she found herself wishing they'd finished the job.

"Boss, she could have the money, you haven't even asked her yet," Carl laughed as he continued rooting through her cabinets. Other than the empty cereal boxes, there was nothing left in the cupboards. She'd sustained herself on ramen and tuna fish for the past few weeks.

Donny chuckled. "Right, right, right." He pressed his hand to his chest and then extended it to her. "Elaine, please take a seat and tell me you've got twenty thousand hidden somewhere in this shitty ass apartment." He leaned back with a wicked smile. "That would make my fucking night."

She pointed at the peanut tin on the floor. Inside, there was a hundred dollars, a hundred dollars she'd desperately wanted to spend on a gift for Lilah, a little something by which she could remember her mom.

One of the new guys—the one who'd taken a hit of cocaine on the way in—bent to the ground and retrieved the tin. He pried it open, chuckled, and showed it to Donny.

"Is this a joke?" Donny said, ripping the tin from his crony's hand and slinging it across the room. It collided with a picture frame propped up on the kitchen counter, shattering the glass across the room. The bills still sat folded inside of it.

Elaine shook her head, trying to keep the tears from clouding her vision.

"Fuck this, Donny. Get on with it already. We gotta pick up that delivery across town in fifteen."

Donny nodded and stood. He rounded the corner toward

Elaine, scratching his beard and assessing her with wicked eyes. She held her breath and watched him reach into his pocket out of the corner of her eye; he was reaching for the switchblade.

She jumped up out of her chair and flew across the room, holding her hands up to keep the four men away from her.

"STOP! I can get you the money."

Donny turned and pounded his fists against the table in anger. "Fucking lies, Elaine!"

The wood threatened to buckle under the force of his fists. She watched it crack in the center, splintering out in two directions. Donny caught his fists just before he rammed them into the table again. He held them aloft and then loosened them, blinking away his anger. He turned toward her and smiled as if the last ten seconds had never happened. She swallowed down her fear as he stepped toward her with the patience of a man stepping toward a scared deer.

"Baby, you can't get me the money. You say that every single time." His voice was soft and comforting, and it scared her more than his shouts. "And you know what happens?" He was so close to her face then, breathing right onto her skin. His warm breath stank from rotted teeth. "You never fucking deliver."

His hand dipped into his pocket for the switchblade and she stood immobile. Her heart hammered in her chest, rioting for her to do something. Act. Move. Run. Instead, she stared up into Donny's dark brown eyes as tears started to flow.

"Please Donny," she choked out through sobs. "Please. This time I really mean it. I know where you can get the money."

Donny laughed and turned back to his men. "You guys hearing this? Maybe she has a few more fuckin' cans of peanuts layin' around."

They chuckled along with him, the sound of it ringing in her ears until Donny flipped open the switchblade and the laughter stopped abruptly. The dull blade caught the light and Elaine finally found the courage to move. She fled past him, trying to make it to the door of the apartment, but he was quicker. He reached out and yanked her by the arm so hard it gave way from the socket.

She screamed in agony as he twisted her back to him, holding the blade right up in the groove of her neck.

"Donny. DONNY, I know this house, I-I-I..." she stammered. "I know when they're not home, I know where they keep everything. Lots of antiques, a-and jewelry and shit."

He laughed in her ear and pressed the blade into her skin, slicing through her like she was made of paper.

"No more fairytales," he bit out.

She squeezed her eyes shut and visualized the brand new TV the Matthews had purchased a few months back. It wasn't worth twenty grand, but it was a start, just a little something to appease Donny until she could think of what to do. Hell, she'd become a whore. She'd strip. She'd go back to selling drugs, anything to stay alive for Lilah.

The blade cut deeper and she felt the rush of blood to her head, pounding with adrenaline and self-preservation.

"WAIT," she pleaded as heavy tears slid down her cheeks. "PLEASE. PLEASE. I'll show you. This house right across town. They'll be gone tomorrow, I swear! They have good stuff, Donny. *Good* stuff."

The pressure of the knife eased up and she inhaled quick, deep breaths.

"We can go first thing tomorrow. I know exactly where they keep the spare key," she promised. "It's a clean job. Super clean job. In and out."

Donny moved the blade and shoved her away. She collided with the edge of the table and groaned as she slid to the ground, sobbing with the relief of getting to live another day.

Donny bent down, edging her chin up with his meaty fingers.

"Elaine, Elaine, shh," he soothed before his tone turned darker. "Stop fucking crying," he snapped.

His grip tightened on her chin, digging painfully into her skin. She forced back tears and blinked up at him.

"Tomorrow is your last chance," he said, his eyes darting back and forth between hers. "Got it?"

She nodded, swallowing down her sobs so he wouldn't yell at her again.

He stood and turned toward the door, and then thought better of it and turned back for her. He pointed the blade at her mouth and his thin lips twisted into a sardonic smirk. "I was going to make it quick and painless, but I want you to know right now: if you're wasting our time with this, I'm going to take my time slicing that pretty face of yours."

He laughed, closed his switchblade, and waved the guys out of her apartment.

CHAPTER FORTY-THREE

Chase

I WAS ABOUT to rip us apart. I knew that by delving into the truth about our mothers' deaths, I was unraveling her world, but I had to pull the string.

"Where was your mom that day, Lilah?" I asked again.

"She was out. I don't know. I never learned all the details." Her gaze shifted back and forth between my eyes as she tried to process the muddled memories in her head. "Why are you doing this?" she asked as tears collected in the corners of her eyes.

I tried to stay calm. My temper raged through me but I couldn't yell. I had to be the calm one.

"She was with them, Lilah. She was the one who let them into our house."

"Stop."

185

I shook my head. The anger was building in my chest, gripping its way around my throat.

"My mom wasn't supposed to be home," I explained. "She was supposed to be at the school carnival, but she ran home for a ladder. Your mom thought they could break in really quick, but that didn't happen."

"Why are you doing this, Chase?" Lilah asked, sorrow seeping through the rage in her eyes.

"She never even tried to stop them!" I yelled.

"Shut up Chase! SHUT UP!" Lilah screamed. Her tough exterior started to strain and crack. "You don't know what you're talking about!"

"She watched her best friend die and she was too cowardly to do anything about it."

"You're a LIAR!" she screamed, gripping her fists around my shirt like she wanted to rip it from my body.

"They strangled my mom and left her for dead," I said as I watched her face.

Her body collapsed against mine. She fell forward and slammed her fists into my chest. Over and over again, she hammered against my chest like a drum. I wrapped my arms around her, holding her up and trying to be strong enough for the both of us. It was useless. I tightened my hold around her elbows so she couldn't move. She tried to claw free of me. I was a human punching bag and Lilah was a wrecking ball.

"Why Chase? Why?" she sobbed.

She kept mumbling into my shirt as she slipped further away from me. Her body stayed right where it was, but I was losing her. My Lilah. She'd always pushed her misplaced anger onto me. Now, she'd forever blame me for being the person to bring the truth to light, for ruining what little respect she still held for her mother.

That blame I could live with. That blame was something I could bear.

CHAPTER FORTY-FOUR

August 2013
Blackwater, Texas

ELAINE WEPT THROUGH most of the night. Hannah was her sister, her guardian angel, and her hero, and in a moment of weakness, Elaine had agreed to rob her blind. Donny had slipped his blade against her neck and instead of slowly descending into darkness, she'd offered up her best friend's house as collateral. It was a new low, even for her.

She kept telling herself that the robbery would be quick and clean. Donny had run through the plan with her a thousand times, but she'd been in a daze, trying to think of a solution out of the whole mess. Even as they stepped into Hannah's backyard and walked up the door, Elaine hadn't given up hope that she'd find some way to make it right.

No one was home. Elaine knew that Hannah and her family were at the summer carnival. Hannah helped organize it every year, so Elaine planned their robbery for 8:00 PM, right smack-dab in the middle of the festivities. Hannah should have been halfway to the top of the Ferris wheel surrounded by funnel cakes and cotton candy.

Elaine noticed the lights on downstairs as she retrieved the spare key from beneath the potted hydrangea out back but didn't think much of it. Hannah tended to leave the lights on even when she wasn't home.

"Hurry up," Donny said, edging behind her and yanking the key out of her hand as Elaine pushed to stand.

He shoved the key into the lock, turned it, and pushed the door open with the care of a destructive giant. Elaine followed Donny and Carl into the house, careful to wipe her shoes on the floor mat. The guys headed for the living room, but Elaine dragged her feet, conscious of the sick feeling pooling in her gut. She wanted to turn and run. She wanted to rewind and go back to the other night and let Donny slide his blade across her neck. Death would be a welcome end to the guilt that grew with every step into that house.

Hannah didn't deserve to be robbed.

She walked past the kitchen, glanced in, and froze when she saw Hannah's purse sitting on the kitchen counter.

Fear gripped her heart as she held out her hand.

"WAIT," she yelled. "Someone's home!"

Donny ignored her and headed for the flat-screen TV hanging on the living room wall.

Elaine shook her head and ran after him, trying to get them to listen. "No. DONNY THEY'RE HOME. LET'S GO."

Carl grabbed her neck and shoved her against the wall

before edging past her to help Donny with the TV.

"Be useful and grab something," Donny said, angling the TV away from the wall mount.

Elaine stepped forward and listened, trying to decide if she heard footsteps upstairs or not. The padded carpet made it impossible to tell.

"I'm going to check upstairs," she said, trying to sound as if her heart wasn't racing a hundred miles a minute.

The guys ignored her. She sprinted up the stairs and paused when the hallway bathroom light flipped off. The door opened and Hannah stepped out, still wiping her hands with a hand towel. She met Elaine's gaze, tilted her head, and frowned.

"Elai—"

Elaine flew forward and pushed her hand over Hannah's mouth, forcing her into silence.

"Don't say a word," she whispered, pleading with her friend to stay silent. "Do you understand?"

Hannah's eyes widened as she tried to break out of Elaine's grasp.

Elaine fought her and pushed them both back into the bathroom. She closed the door and kept the light off. The two of them stood in darkness as Elaine listened to determine whether the guys had heard them. Two long seconds passed in silence and then Elaine moved her hand away from Hannah's mouth.

"Someone's in my house?" Hannah whispered.

"Yes. Two men. Two very bad men." Elaine paused and turned toward the door, listening for Donny and Carl. They were yelling at each other downstairs but she couldn't make out their words. She turned back to Hannah and grabbed her arms. "Let them rob you. I'll buy you a new TV. I'll buy you a new house. Hannah, just please stay in here and don't say a word."

Hannah reached out and gripped Elaine's arms in the darkness. "What are you doing, Elaine? Are you *helping* them?"

Elaine shook her head over and over again. "I'll explain it all, I promise, just please—"

"ELAINE. Where are you?" Donny yelled from the foot of the stairs.

Hannah jumped and let out a little squeak. In the quiet bathroom it sounded as if she'd just yelled bloody murder, but Elaine had to hope Donny hadn't heard. She put her hand up to Hannah's mouth and pressed her index finger against her lips before turning for the door. She cracked it open and yelled down for him.

"Donny, I'm up here looking through jewelry."

"Well fuckin' hurry up and get back down here," he yelled.

Elaine swallowed and closed the door as quietly as possible. She turned back to Hannah and heard rustling in the darkness. Then she felt a cold chain brush her arm, and then another, and another. Hannah was holding out something for her to take and when Elaine reached for it, she felt a tangle of necklaces. Hannah was holding out her jewelry for Elaine to take and the realization cracked Elaine's black heart in two.

"Take them," Hannah said, forcing them out to her friend. "Take them. They should be worth a little."

Elaine shook her head as the sadness in her gut shifted to her chest. She felt the tears stain her cheeks before she could stop them. She didn't want to be this person. She didn't want to steal from Hannah.

"Elaine," Hannah whispered. "Take them. We'll figure this out."

Elaine wiped the tears from her cheeks as she tried to think of what to do. There had to be a way out. She didn't want Hannah's jewelry, she didn't want Hannah's TV. She wanted freedom; she wanted a new life.

"Elaine. We'll figure it out," Hannah repeated, tugging her friend into a tight hug and shoving the necklaces into her hand. The cold metal burned Elaine's palm as she cried into Hannah's hair. Hannah gripped her tighter, holding her up and soothing her.

"This isn't you. I know this isn't you right now," Hannah assured her. "Now go."

The more Hannah tried to soothe her, the more inconsolable Elaine became. She wanted Hannah to pull her out of the nightmare, to take her hand and drag her out of the darkness. She opened her mouth to plead for help, but it was too late. Donny had crested the top of the stairs before she could get the words out. Elaine heard his footsteps in the hallway and she lunged to lock the bathroom door just before Donny's boot kicked it open. The door slammed against the wall, punching a hole in the drywall.

Elaine backed up, trying to conceal Hannah behind her as Donny stood silhouetted by the light from the hallway.

"You fucking whore," he yelled, bounding forward and shoving Elaine into the wall. She winced as sharp pain radiated through her shoulder.

"Was this your plan all along?" he asked, crowding over her. His spit flew into her eyes and his boot held down her chest, threatening to break her ribs. "Get yourself a little witness so you could pin the robbery on us and then slip away like a little rat?"

She tried to push away from the wall, but Donny reached down and yanked her up by the throat. His meaty fingers closed in around her windpipe and her vision blurred. Black shadows loomed in the corners of her eyes as she fought him off, scraping at his fingers and kicking at him as hard as she could.

"LET HER GO," Hannah screamed, holding out her cell phone to show that she'd placed a call to 911. The call rang twice before a dispatcher picked up on the other end.

"911, what city?" the dispatcher spoke from the receiver.

"LET HER GO AND LEAVE," Hannah yelled.

Donny's grip loosened around Elaine's throat as he turned his sights on Hannah.

She braced herself and held the phone out toward him with a shaky hand.

"Leave right now and I'll hang up the phone," she declared with a confident voice.

"Hello? 911, what's your emergency?" the dispatcher repeated.

Hannah held the phone to her ear, frantically trying to get out their address. "Send the police to 145—"

Donny backhanded the phone out of her grasp. It flew against the bathroom mirror, splintering the cheap glass into a million pieces. Shards rained down over them as Donny shoved Hannah to the ground. He pinned her stomach down with his knee as he reached for her neck.

Elaine coughed and forced breath back into her lungs, trying to regain the strength to save her friend. Hannah's phone was lying a few feet away from her. She reached out for it, slicing her hand on the shards of glass as she pressed buttons, trying to reconnect the call. The screen was black and cracked down the center, too broken to be fixed.

Hannah struggled and screamed, trying to land a solid punch to Donny's face as he strangled her. She thrashed like a fish out of water, clawing at his eyes and digging her nails into his face.

Elaine grabbed a half-empty perfume bottle on the bathroom counter and chunked it at the back of Donny's head. She jumped onto his back, hammering her fists into his head, trying desperately to pull his attention back to her. She scratched at his eyes and screamed at him through her sobs.

"GET OFF HER!"

She could handle his blows, she could take his punishment, but she couldn't watch Hannah's face turn purple beneath Donny's grip.

"Please, Donny, please," she begged, pounding against him. "STOP!"

She felt a pair of hands yank her off him and felt Carl overpower her. She recognized his arm around her throat and his mouth against her ear. His dark words warned her to stay put, to cooperate and make it easy.

She knew she was helpless to save her best friend and yet she couldn't give up.

She stared at Hannah's hazel eyes as they bulged, reddened, and began to dim.

She yanked at the hold Carl had on her, crying and screaming for them to stop. They had to stop. They had to listen.

"PLEASE!" she yelled, digging her nails into Carl's arm and carrying away strips of skin.

He hissed in her ear and reared back to punch her in the side, right above her kidney. Sharp, blaring pain radiated through Elaine's body, but she was numb to the sensation. She could have been sliced in two, right down the middle, and it would have hurt less than watching her best friend die before her eyes.

Donny's grip stole the breath from Hannah's lungs without thought or remorse, like a gust of wind taking a flame from a match. Elaine watched from two feet away as Hannah's body slowly, slowly deflated.

Everything was loud, so deafeningly loud as Elaine's screams ricocheted around the bathroom, and then there was no sound at all.

There was nothing.

Hannah was dead and she'd taken Elaine's senses with her.

Carl and Donny scrambled from the bathroom and Elaine crawled toward Hannah's lifeless body.

She felt nothing as her fingertips skimmed across her best friend's pale cheek. She saw nothing as she gripped Hannah's body and pulled her up, trying to shake her back to life. She tasted nothing as her salty tears coated her lips. She heard nothing as she whispered for her friend to come back to her. She could smell nothing, not the sweat coating her body or the spilled perfume coating the bathroom floor.

She needed to follow Hannah. She belonged with her in life and in death. They were entwined deeper than lovers and more intimately than family. Without Hannah to guide her, Elaine was a lost soul. She hovered in the twilight of life, begging for death so she could join her friend. Heaven or hell, it didn't matter.

She'd cling to Hannah anywhere, *always*.

CHAPTER FORTY-FIVE

Lilah

I WANTED HIS words to be a lie. I wanted my life to stay neatly packaged. I wanted to wake up every morning and pretend that my mother, even with her problems, still had her redeeming qualities. Now, I had nothing left to cling to. Chase had ripped that away from me like he was ripping stitches from a fresh wound. Without the delusions to keep together, I was forced to remember the last time I'd ever seen my mom alive.

She had gone missing after Hannah's death, but somehow I had known she'd be at Hannah's funeral. Everyone had gathered at the Matthews' house so that close family and friends could share in their memories of Hannah's life.

My mother arrived like a tornado. She was impossible to miss as she stormed in crying and screaming at all of us.

The image of her oily skin and yellowed teeth haunted me. She looked nothing like the woman who'd tried to raise me for seven years before calling it quits. She looked wild, like a feral animal.

"You don't understand! None of you understand!" she screamed, flailing her arms out, trying to get someone to listen. "It wasn't supposed to happen!"

She staggered down the back stairs, sobbing incoherently, but the second her eyes locked on me, her insane delirium seemed to lessen.

"Lilah, come give your mom a hug. I miss you so much, baby," she crooned, stumbling over her own feet as she tried to reach me.

Chase stood up and put his body in front of mine. Even at sixteen he was bigger than she was.

"Don't you dare come near her," he threatened. "My mom wouldn't want you here! I don't want you here!"

She kept trying to come closer and I sidestepped Chase to get to her. She was my mom, but Chase wouldn't let me get by him. He held his arm out to block me.

"We don't want you here! This is your fault! You did this to her!" he yelled, and finally his words started to sink in for her.

She stopped her pursuit to get to me, a blank zombie stare tainting her bright green eyes.

My dad and Mr. Matthews rushed out of the back door trailed by two police officers.

"Elaine, what are you doing here?" my dad yelled.

Mr. Matthews bypassed the pleasantries. "Get the hell out of here! So help me god, if you don't get out of this house, I will kill you myself!"

I'd never heard Mr. Matthews yell in my life, but he wouldn't stop. He yelled at my mom to get out over and over again until I started to scream at him to stop.

My dad wrapped a hand around my mom's bicep and pulled her through the side gate before Chase or his dad lost it even more. I was in a daze, trying to comprehend the fact that I'd just seen my mother for the first time in a year and she'd looked like she was on the brink of death. Her sunken cheeks belonged on a skeleton, not the woman that had given birth to me.

The police officers followed them out of the yard and pulled out their handcuffs. They were trying to arrest her, but she struggled, screaming at them to let her go.

"Chase, let me get to her. Let me get to her!" I yelled, trying to shove him away. I needed her. With Mrs. Matthews gone, I needed my mom even more, but Chase wouldn't let me go. He held on to me so tightly, his fingers leaving marks on my arms, my screams doing nothing to deter him.

They pulled my mother toward the police cruiser as she dragged her feet, wailing for them to let her go. I had to watch them cart her away and I broke down in sobs, completely helpless to save her.

The sick memory of that day faded as Chase repeated my name over and over again on the stairs. Reality sank in like a sharp knife and I looked up into Chase's hazel eyes, trying to find reason within the chaos.

"You wouldn't let me near her. I wanted to hug her so badly. She needed me and I couldn't get to her." I dropped my head and let the tears fall. "After everything, I just wanted her to go back to being my mom again."

"I'm sorry."

He couldn't have known that'd be the last time I'd ever see her. He couldn't have known how important that moment would become in my life. My emotions had been stirred up with the grief of having to say goodbye to Mrs. Matthews. I had been mourning her death when my own mother decided to show up and make everything so much worse. I'd needed someone I could pin my anger on for the unfairness of it all, and I'd chosen the one person who could take it: Chase.

I stared up into his eyes, expecting to find anger. Instead, there was only grief. He hadn't been given the chance to say goodbye to his mom either.

"I'm so sorry she took your mom away from you, Chase," I said, stepping away from him. I knew tears were slipping down my cheeks but I was numb to their touch.

I should have known there was even more my mother had to atone for. It wasn't enough to ruin her own family, she had to ruin Chase's family too.

"She didn't kill her, Lilah. At sixteen, I was angry and sad. I wanted to blame someone and when I saw your mom, I just reacted."

I shook my head. He was so wrong. "Your mom wouldn't have been killed if... She was just so consumed with her own demons, she was blind to everyone else."

"We'll never know, Lilah. There's no point in holding on to that anger."

I inhaled a shaky breath, feeling the sadness well up inside me even more.

"Your mom was good. She didn't deserve to die."

Chase stayed silent for a long while and when he finally spoke, his voice was calm and resolute. "I've had two years to think about that night, and I've truly come to believe that my mom would still have gone back to the house even if she'd known what would happen to her. That night didn't just happen the way it did because of your mom's need for salvation. It was just as much a result of my mom's need to be her savior."

There was so much misplaced blame surrounding our mothers' deaths.

The only thing I could do was take a deep breath and realize that I'd been looking at the situation from one perspective. For years, Chase had been the scapegoat for my grief. As I stepped back, I realized Chase wasn't at fault. Through some alchemy, he'd found a way to turn his hate, blame, anger, and sadness into forgiveness. Now, he had shown me how as well. The blame I'd harbored for him could be deflated and thrown away. Just like that.

Poof.

Gone.

CHAPTER FORTY-SIX

August 2013
Blackwater, Texas

ELAINE DIDN'T KNOW where she was going, but she'd been running all her life. Her body knew what to do; she was built to flee. Her feet hammered against the pavement. Left, right, left, right. She'd lost her breath a mile back, but the sobs kept coming, ripping through her like they were trying to tear her in two.

She'd already lived a week without her friend, she wouldn't last much longer. The police would find her and haul her back to jail. She'd have to deal with Donny's people on the inside.

It will never end.

Lilah would never have the mother she deserved. She'd

spend her weekends visiting Elaine in jail, wasting her spare change on the vending machine in the visitor's room.

It will never end.

She hadn't slept since Hannah's death. Every time she swallowed, she was reminded of the raw flesh of Donny's grip around her throat.

It will never end.

She was done with the suffering.

She would make it end.

CHAPTER FORTY-SEVEN

Lilah

SATURDAY MORNING I found myself standing outside Blackwater Cemetery. I leaned on the wrought iron fence, dropped my chin to my arms, and counted down the row of gravestones until I landed on the one tenth from the left and five from the back. That was where Hannah Matthews had been buried a few months before my mother had taken the plot beside her, just like they'd requested.

They'd had wills drawn up before Chase and I were born that detailed their wishes after death. The wills had been short and silly, the result of two eighteen-year-olds trying to plan for an event they'd assumed would be seventy-years in the making. The concise instructions dictated their wishes to rest beside one another, two gravestones with a three-word epitaph. I didn't need to see the front of their gravestones to remember the three words chiseled in memory of their lives.

Mother. Wife. Friend.

Three words inscribed in that order. At eighteen, they'd been young, pregnant, and in love with our fathers. Those three words seemed fitting, but now it all seemed like a cruel joke. Hannah's words were correct, but out of order. Her epitaph should have read: Friend. Mother. Wife. After all, it was her unyielding friendship with my mother that had killed her in the end.

While Hannah's words were out of order, my mother's were just plain wrong. She wasn't a mother, wife, or friend. I stared at the back of her gravestone and wished I could scrape off the lies inscribed on the other side. Chase had shown me how to forgive the living, but I couldn't bring myself to absolve the dead.

The seed of sadness Chase had planted on the stairs the night before had bloomed into full-blown grief overnight. The details he'd revealed had torn open a wound that had never managed to heal properly in the first place. The bandages were rotten and so easy to tear.

I'd gone two years thinking I was fine, even *relieved* that my mom was gone, but as I stared at the back of her gravestone, rage boiled deep inside me.

I had thought you couldn't be mad at a ghost.

I had thought once someone died, it'd be hard to look back in anger.

I'd been so wrong.

You can be mad at a ghost. You can be so royally pissed at a ghost that your entire body feels like a live wire about to explode.

I felt for the camera hanging around my neck—the one Chase had given me—and I focused the lens at the back of my mother's gravestone. I adjusted the exposure and zoomed in. I pressed down and the shutter snapped, breaking up the silence of the cemetery.

Chase had given me the camera so I could use it like a private investigator, but my very first photo wasn't taken to uncover other people's secrets, it was to acknowledge my own.

• • •

I took the long way home from the cemetery, thinking over my confrontation with Chase. By the time I walked through my front door, it was well past dinnertime. I peeked into the kitchen, relieved to discover that the person scribbling at the table was my dad, not Chase. I couldn't confront Chase yet. I felt like a glass vase teetering on the edge of a table; one soft breeze and I'd scatter across the floor into a million sharp pieces.

The soft glow of the overhead light cast my dad's face into shadows. His head dipped forward as he jotted down notes onto a yellow legal pad. One glance from across the room and I knew he was working on baseball stats. It was his own form of therapy—everything was right in the world whenever he had a yellow legal pad.

I watched him run his hand through his thick salt and pepper hair, and then he finally glanced up at me as I rounded the table toward him.

"Hey, Lil, I was just about to call and see where you were. Are you hungry?" he asked, dropping his ballpoint pen on top of the legal pad with a thud and scooting his chair back against the hardwood floor.

I held up my hand to stop him from standing up. "No. I'll try to eat something in the morning." My stomach was too knotted for food.

His brows scrunched together. "Is something wrong? You look pale."

I didn't want to talk about it, but I had to know the truth. It would have been easier to turn and run, but instead, I pulled out the dining chair in front of me and sat down. Unable to meet his eyes, I said the words slowly. "I'm still mad at mom for what she did to Hannah."

I took a deep breath and looked up. In a matter of a couple seconds, my father's entire demeanor shifted. He closed his eyes and heaved a sigh before rocking back to rest against the spine of his chair.

"Your mother had a complicated life, Lilah. I'm sure you know bits and pieces of it, but she came from a deeply troubled home. When your grandfather had been drinking, your mom would run over to Hannah's house. She was your mom's escape, but as they got older, their relationship wasn't healthy any more. I think part of the reason your mom never changed her ways was because she knew Hannah would always be there to pick up the pieces."

I'd heard hints of my mother's abusive childhood, but my father had never spelled it out as clearly as that before.

"Chase said Mrs. Matthews would have gone back home that day even if she'd known what was going to happen." I wanted him to solidify the fact.

He frowned. "There's no telling what might've happened if several things had been different in our lives. Looking for someone to blame doesn't bring anyone back, Lilah."

A calm anger rolled through me and I reached out to grab the edge of the table. If my mother was still alive I would have gripped her shoulders through her jail cell bars and shaken her body until she screamed at me to stop. How can someone be so evil? So selfish? How could she not care more about her only friend?

I turned away from him to look out the back door. Without the porch light on, I could see parts of my reflection in the windowpanes.

"Did they ever find the guys who killed her?" I asked as I stared at my reflection.

"Yes."

"Do you think Mom helped identify the person?"

He nodded and chewed on his bottom lip. "I know she did."

With a deep breath, I stood up from my chair and rounded the table. I didn't want any more answers. That was enough for one day. My dad wrapped his strong arms around my shoulders and I sunk into the crook of his neck. He smelled like home, a familiar woodsy scent that I'd missed in Austin.

I whispered against his hair. "I love you, Dad."

"I love you too, Lil. I don't tell you enough." He squeezed me tighter before releasing me.

I stood up and wiped the tears from my face. I was headed out of the kitchen when I thought of one last question.

"Dad."

I spun around to find him watching me with sad eyes.

"Do you think...I'm like her?"

It was a loaded question. Part of me wanted nothing to do with the woman.

He smiled softly. "You have all of her best qualities. When I first met her, she was beautiful and kind. She was truly a brilliant woman."

I nibbled on the side of my mouth.

"Does that help?"

I shook my head, trying to clear my head. "I'm not sure

yet."

CHAPTER FORTY-EIGHT

Chase

LILAH WAS NOWHERE to be found on Saturday morning. I knocked on her door and let Harvey into her room to scope it out for me. He came back with one of her socks in his mouth, very proud of himself for accomplishing such a stealthy recon mission. *Some help you are.*

We had the week off of baseball, so I lingered around the house all day, fixing cameras with my door open. I angled my chair against my desk, set out my tools, and peeked into the hallway whenever I thought I heard footsteps on the stairs. By the end of the day, I was convinced the Calloways' house was haunted—either that or I was going crazy.

Around dinnertime, I headed downstairs and found Coach seasoning meat for tacos.

"Have you seen Lilah?" he asked, peering over his

shoulder at me.

I shook my head. "Not since last night."

He nodded and turned back to the stove. We both knew there was no point in worrying. Lilah would come back when she was ready and not a second before.

After dinner, I showered, packed up my cameras and tools, and then pulled *The Stranger* out of my backpack. I climbed in bed, pulled out my bookmark, and propped myself against the pillows as I started to read. Harvey was by my side and I was absentmindedly petting him while I flipped through the pages of the novel. I didn't have a clue what time it was when I heard a light tapping on my door.

"Chase, are you awake?" Lilah whispered.

Harvey peered up at me with tired eyes, clearly annoyed at being awoken from his beauty sleep.

"Lilah?" I threw the blankets off and sat up. "Yeah, I'm awake."

The door creaked open and then Lilah slowly stepped through wearing pajama shorts and a tank top. I swallowed and pulled my gaze to her face.

"What's wrong?"

Her eyes were downcast.

"I'm really sorry, Chase."

I swiveled my legs off the side of my bed. "Lilah, no, you don't have to be sorry."

She crossed her arms and scanned the room around me. There wasn't much to look at, but I guess anything was better than meeting my eyes. *What is she so afraid of?*

"I've spent all day thinking about it..." she admitted with a meek tone. "And I don't know where to go from here."

At times I wondered if Lilah and I were buried too deep in our pasts to ever work out. There were layers that had to be completely demolished before we could get to anything real, and at some point, there would be an end to us. Whether it was an end I'd be happy with, I couldn't be sure.

"Do you want to talk about something else instead?" I asked, trying my damnedest to unlock the secrets of Lilah Calloway.

She nibbled on her bottom lip and shook her head.

"How about I talk?" I asked, making sure my voice was low enough that we wouldn't wake up her dad.

She nodded and took a step closer to the bed. Harvey sat up, hopeful that she'd come closer and pet him. I pushed him farther down so that he was at the foot of the bed.

"C'mon," I told Lilah, patting the pillow next to mine.

She moved quickly as if relieved by my invitation to lie down beside me. I watched her round the bed and slip under the covers, bringing the smell of her shampoo with her. I inhaled deeply and then burrowed down beside her. When our eyes met, she smiled, small and simple.

"Okay, so what should I talk about?"

Without missing a beat, she answered, "Memories of your mom."

I felt a slight sting in my chest, like someone grazing my heart with the edge of a knife. I thought about my mom every day, but I hardly ever talked about her.

Lilah sensed my unease. "Do you remember the time she pulled us out of school and took us to the beach? I think we were ten or eleven at the time."

I smiled at the memory. My mom had told our teachers we'd both had doctor's appointments and they hadn't questioned her.

"She took us down to Port Aransas, but she hadn't realized how long it would take."

Lilah laughed. "It was like a six hour car ride just to get there."

"But the beach was deserted."

"And the waves were really big."

I nodded, recalling the buried memories. "That was such a fun day."

"Do you remember how jealous our dads were when we told them about it?" She smiled, and we began a slow descent into memories. We told story after story about my mom and our childhood. It felt good to reminisce and I knew it was making Lilah happy. Her features relaxed and the demons that had haunted her all day seemed to have disappeared at the door. I watched her talk, loving the shape of her mouth and the words that slipped out of it. I almost told her how I felt; the declaration was on the tip of my tongue.

Lilah, I love you.

Instead, I scooted closer and whispered another story to her, her eyes focused on mine as she absorbed every word.

I wasn't sure who fell asleep first, but I woke up in the middle of the night with her hand on my chest and my heart in her palm. With her and Harvey in bed with me, it felt like I had everything I ever wanted, even if it was just for a moment.

I stayed up and watched her for a little while, studying the slope of her cheekbones and the small pout of her lips. She had delicate features and when she slept, they relaxed into perfect symmetry.

Just before I drifted off, a thought spiraled through me, gripping hold of my mind until all hope for sleep wasted away.

The relationship I used to have with Lilah is gone. She isn't my childhood friend any more, and if I lose her this time, it will be forever.

CHAPTER FORTY-NINE

Chase

THE SUN BEAT down on the pitcher's mound as I checked first base. The runner was anxious to edge farther from the bag, but he stayed put. I turned to the batter, reared back, and threw a curveball. The ball sped through the air, the batter swung and missed, and the ball slammed into the catcher's mitt with a loud clap.

"OUT!"

The crowd went wild. I'd just pitched the best game of my life: 9 strikeouts and only one earned run. I slipped off my glove as my teammates rushed to meet me on the mound. I smiled and went through the motions, but I couldn't ignore the fact that my dad wasn't in the stands. He'd promised he'd be there. It was the last game before playoffs, and he'd sworn to me that he'd come out to watch

214

it.

Lilah was there, just like she'd been at all the games since the start of the season. She didn't sit with the Diamond Girls; she perched up at the top of the bleachers with her hat pulled low over her face. It was awkward giving a rose to Kimberly at the end of every game, but it wasn't as if I had a choice. Every player gave a rose; it was tradition, and Kimberly was a good friend. She didn't deserve to be ditched just because I loved Lilah.

I'd taken to buying a dozen roses at the supermarket before every game on the off chance Lilah stayed to talk to me after the game. I didn't really blame her for leaving. The flowers were starting to pile up on the bench seat of my truck, dried out and wilting. The clerk who rang up my orders always eyed my uniform suspiciously, but I didn't pay him any mind. One day Lilah would stay and it would be worth the trouble.

I hopped into my truck, not bothering with a shower or a change of clothes. I pushed the roses to the passenger side and then drove straight to my dad's house. There was no telling what kind of state he'd be in when I arrived, but I exhaled as I saw his car parked next to an old red Firebird I didn't recognize.

At least he's home.

I pulled up behind his car in the driveway and cut the engine, running through my mental rolodex of cars. I couldn't place the Firebird—at least, no one came to mind. I tucked my keys into my pocket and moved to get out, but then the screen door creaked to life. I peered through the front window as a woman stumbled out of the front door looking like she had seen better days. Her hair was short and bleached, and her skin was tanned and leathery. The heels of her shoes sunk into the grass as she walked, so she held her arms out like a tightrope walker trying to steady herself.

After nearly face planting a few times, she finally made it to her car, never noticing me sitting in my truck in the driveway.

I waited two minutes after her Firebird peeled away before walking into the house. I patted my jeans to make sure my keys were in my front pocket. There was a chance I'd need to bolt, especially if my dad was drunk.

I pulled the frayed screen door open and tapped my knuckles on the wood frame.

"Dad, are you in here?" I called out to the quiet house. The carpet was stained with yellow and brown patches and there was trash covering the coffee table. Pill bottles lay beside cigarette packs and empty coke cans.

I peered into the kitchen just as the toilet flushed in the guest bathroom downstairs. I turned as my father walked out, zipping up his jeans. When he caught sight of me, he paused and narrowed his eyes as if trying to figure out if I was really there.

"When did you get here?" he asked with a gruff voice before stepping past me and taking a seat on the couch. The old springs collapsed under his weight.

"Just now," I said, pointing toward the door. "I saw your friend leave." I could have skirted around the subject, but I was tired of skirting around subjects with him.

He grunted and reached down to light a cigarette. I reached forward and grabbed the pack before he could.

"Don't smoke around me," I said, tossing the pack across the room so that it hit the wall and tumbled to the ground, spilling cigarettes onto the floor.

"What the hell has gotten into you, boy?" he asked, a dark gleam in his eye.

I was one bold move away from pushing him too far, so I backtracked and took a deep breath.

"I wanted to come see how you were doing," I said, taking a seat in the chair across from him. I couldn't smell the sweat of my uniform over the musk lingering in the room. The place was disgusting.

"I'm fine," he nodded, reclining back and propping his arms on the back of the couch.

"Have you been down to the shop lately?"

His eyes were pinned on something outside as he answered. "Once or twice last week. Been slow."

I nodded and dropped my hands between my legs. "How are you paying for things?"

His eyes cut to me. "Y'know, I don't appreciate being lectured by a fucking eighteen-year-old boy, even if you are my son."

I laughed under my breath. "You think it's fun having to lecture my dad?"

He grunted and I knew we were at a standstill, so I decided to drop the subject.

He reached forward and took a sip of cheap beer, no doubt lukewarm by that point.

"I had a baseball game today," I mentioned, finding middle ground.

"Yeah, how'd that go?" he asked, eyeing my uniform.

"We won. We're headed to the first round of playoffs."

He nodded in approval. "That's really somethin'. Maybe I'll try to make it to the next game."

His promise meant nothing. I reclined back in the chair, feeling the lump of my phone in my back pocket. I would have removed it, but I wasn't sure how much longer I'd be staying.

"How's Calloway treating ya?" he asked, taking another

sip of beer.

I twisted my hands together. "Fine."

"Getting close with that daughter of his again?" he asked with a gentle sneer.

"Her name is Lilah," I said firmly, straightening up in my seat.

My dad grunted again and it took everything inside me not to reach out and smack the beer from his hand. I watched him lean forward, his hazel eyes locking onto mine. His skin was oily and wrinkled. I wondered when he'd last showered.

"I'd be careful with her," he warned, narrowing his eyes.

"What are you talking about?"

He dragged his tongue along his bottom lip, gathering his thoughts. "She always reminded me a little too much of her mother…"

"Just say what you want to say," I hissed.

"Her mom was a stupid whore and the apple doesn't fall far from the tree."

I gripped the edge of my chair.

"You don't know a single thing about her," I argued.

"I know she's trouble," he said, reaching for the pack of cigarettes.

"You. Don't. Know. Her."

"Do you think the two of you together is a good idea?" He tried to get his lighter to spark, striking it three times before it finally lit. He took a long drag and then met my eye once again. "Our families are so mangled and tangled up, ain't nothin' good can come from it."

"She's a good person."

He shook his head and pointed his finger out at me, flicking ash across the carpet. "Yeah, Elaine seemed like a good person when she was 17 too. Maybe she doesn't have problems now, but she will. You just wait."

I thought of the version of Lilah that had returned from Austin: the closed-off girl with her black hair and flat smile, the girl who tried her best to hide away from the world. I knew it wouldn't happen overnight, but I could get the old Lilah back. I could find the lost girl.

"You're just spouting hateful bullshit now," I said with a steely confidence. "You know how I know you're wrong?"

My dad arched a brow in response.

"Because I'm nothing like you," I said with a sharp tongue. "Lilah won't turn into her mom because I'm sure as hell not gonna turn into you. Look at yourself." I sneered. "You're a forty-year-old man drinking yourself into oblivion. You lost your wife, and I lost my mom. You can't just pretend that life doesn't go on." I shook my head. "Why can't you see that? Why can't you see that you've turned a sad thing into something even worse? I couldn't mourn the death of my mom because I was too busy making sure you didn't choke on your own vomit every night."

I stood and pulled the keys out of my uniform pocket. The entire walk to the front door was met with silence from my father, but I wasn't under the delusion that he'd listened to a single word.

Drunk bastards don't change.

CHAPTER FIFTY

Lilah

SECRETS MAKE UP the backbone of a small town. Secrets, gossip, and lies. No one cops up to it. Sweet-looking old biddies talk shit about their friends, but follow it up with a "bless her heart" and everyone pretends it's all right. It doesn't matter if you try and dress it up with a pretty bow; gossip is gossip is gossip, and I loved every juicy piece I could get.

The secrets piled up faster than I could scribble them into my journal. They were like weeds growing out of control with no one to keep them in check. I hoarded them, coating my new journal with them until the black ink bled across every page.

My small town was hiding more than I could have ever hoped. There was fraud: the Baptist church downtown hadn't been a victim of faulty wiring; the church elders had set it ablaze for the insurance money. There were affairs and adultery: everyone from a teacher's aide at my high school to Mr. Hill across the street. Cheaters were sloppy and indulgent. Most of them wanted to be caught, but they were too weak to come right out and admit it. There were small secrets—neighbors watering their lawns during drought restrictions—and big secrets—D&T bakery downtown was a cozy little front for a money laundering drug operation.

Most of the time, the secrets fell in my lap, but in other cases I had to do some investigating. I sat in D&T bakery after school, watching and listening. The first time there was a money drop, I didn't believe I'd actually seen it. I had to go back three more times before I actually confirmed my suspicions. Stuffed in between the chocolate croissants and glazed bear claws were thousands of dollars of dirty drug money. I had always wondered what the workers at a 24-hour bakery did during the 20 hours of downtime.

I scribbled down every secret I could find, exposing my journal pages to the liars of Blackwater, Texas, and every lie I scribbled down helped soothe my soul.

Listening to the town's gossip had its disadvantages though; I heard every murmured word about Chase and me. I saw every lip that was pursed and every take that doubled.

"Chase has such a bright future, and she's so troubled. Bless her heart."

I wanted to kill the next person who tried to bless my heart.

"What does he see in her?"

I wished I could have answered them, "I have no idea."

I flipped through the pages of my journal, running my hand over the words I'd scribbled there the day before. I didn't want to go home, so I sat inside D&T and pretended not to notice when someone ordered the blackcurrant macaroons, an inconspicuous off-menu item.

The bell chimed over the door and I glanced up to see Kimberly's parents, Mr. and Mrs. White, walk into the bakery with big smiles. I hadn't seen them in years, but they'd aged like vampires: no wrinkles, no worries, just perfect smiles and bright blue eyes.

Mrs. White scanned the small space until her eyes landed on me.

"Lilah Calloway! What a surprise," she said, skimming her gaze down my Jake Bugg t-shirt and dark jeans. "I haven't seen you since you and Kimberly's dancing days."

I closed my journal and slid it off the table, offering up a fake smile as they approached. "Yeah, it's been a while."

Mr. White stood behind her, beaming down at me from ear to ear. *Ever the smiling dentist.*

"How have you been?" she asked.

"Fine."

My lackluster conversational skills didn't deter her.

"Kimberly mentioned that you and Chase were seeing each other," Mrs. White said with a tilt of her head. "You know, I have to say that we always had Chase picked out for Kimberly. I mean the two of them were so inseparable...while you were away."

Her hollow eyes made it impossible to tell if she was being malicious or just oblivious. Still, I wanted to reach up and clamp my hand over her mouth. I didn't need to hear stories about Kimberly and Chase. I had a running loop of their happy faces constantly playing in my head.

"We aren't really together," I offered awkwardly.

Her eyes filled with hope. "Oh? Kimberly was just *infatuated* with him for the longest time. We used to laugh when she'd spend hours getting ready for one of their dates."

"Oh, that's funny," I said, flashing her a flat smile, hoping she'd take the hint and leave. She didn't. For all I knew, I'd be stuck talking to them for the rest of the afternoon.

"I heard Chase has had quite a few offers to play college ball. Isn't that amazing?" She didn't give me time to confirm that it was 'amazing'. "Do you have plans for after graduation?"

I narrowed my eyes, knowing full well that Mrs. White didn't care about me. She'd never called after the funeral or offered to help our family. She wanted to know what I was doing so she could compare it to Kimberly. She needed validation that she was a good parent and that Kimberly was the popular little princess she'd always wanted to raise.

I stood and relinquished the table I'd occupied for the last hour. I scooted around them and tipped my imaginary hat.

"Y'know, the only thing I know for sure is that I'm getting the hell out of this town."

Their mouths dropped and I offered a wave.

"I've gotta run, but enjoy your dessert. I'd probably go for the cupcakes if I were you."

The cupcakes were safe. They were fluffy, innocent desserts. It was the blackcurrant macaroons that signaled a buy.

• • •

When I got home from the bakery, I went out to inspect the progress of my garden with Harvey by my side. The plants were growing like mad, overtaking the beds and soaking up every drop of water I gave them. I dropped the hose in one of the beds and headed for my raspberry vines. I'd planted four bushes along the fence line so the vines could climb up around the wooden planks. The raspberries were growing slowly, on their own terms. Out of all my plants, I was most like those raspberries vines.

I ran my finger along the budding vines and then forced myself to finish watering the rest of the garden. Once every bed was soaked, I kicked off my shoes and went in to feed Harvey an early dinner. My dad wasn't home from the baseball game yet and the house was too quiet; there was nothing to help drown out the negative thoughts overtaking my mind. I leaned against the counter and replayed my conversation with Mrs. White until I couldn't stand it any longer.

I hated Mrs. White, but she wasn't the only one who didn't want me to end up with Chase. It confused everyone. It ruined their perfect image of what life should be. Chase was supposed to marry a prom queen, take over the Blackwater Ford dealership, and run for city government. Me? I was supposed to turn into my mother.

It wasn't a novel idea; I thought about the possibility of becoming her every single day. It was easy to see the similarities, but every time I indulged myself, my logic would eventually kick in. I wasn't her. I knew that. Still, people viewed me as her spawn. I'd been branded as trouble from the start.

I was standing at my bedroom window, contemplating the opinions of my small town when Chase's truck pulled up into the driveway. I watched him hop out and my heart kicked up a notch, an innate reaction to his presence. He looked up to see me standing in the window and waved before picking up the pace to get inside.

I kept my gaze on the spot where he'd stood smiling up at me and tried to shove down the secret clawing its way to the front of my thoughts. Loving Chase wasn't a choice. Every day, I rubbed the sleep from my eyes, took a deep breath, and shouldered the weight of my love for him. Even after everything we'd been through, that was my biggest secret, the one I tried to drown in my journal.

I loved the golden boy. I woke up loving him and I drifted to sleep loving him, but having that love returned, letting that love blossom wasn't a possibility. Even if we could work our way through our past, no one thought I was good enough for him—and honestly, I wasn't.

When I heard Chase open the front door and bound up the stairs, my excitement to see him momentarily displaced the sadness. My door knob twisted and I turned to find him standing in my doorway with a broad smile.

"What are you doing?" I asked.

He took a moment to catch his breath, his broad chest rising and falling beneath his jersey.

"I saw you at my game. Just like I've seen you at all the games."

I crossed my arms and shrugged. "It's not a big deal. I don't have anything else to do on Saturday afternoons."

Chase smirked and pushed off the door with dangerous intent.

I held up my hands to stop him, but I knew it was a worthless attempt. "I can smell you from all the way over here!"

He smiled wider and stepped close. "Is your dad home?"

I swallowed. "No."

He reached out for my waist, gripping it in his hands and tugging me against him.

"Chase, my dad will flip," I said, pretending I was more concerned about my dad coming home than Chase's hands on my hips.

He dipped down to kiss my cheek, his fingers spinning slow circles along my lower back, driving me mad.

"I thought you said he wasn't home."

I was slipping away. Chase was...

"I—"

My thoughts and speech jumbled together into a mess of inaction. I wanted to push him away, to remind myself of the facts, but Chase's lips were on my cheek and my neck and then they hovered over mine, waiting for my permission so gently I thought I would crumble.

"You stink," I teased, trying to lighten the moment.

He laughed and took a step back, lifting his uniform up and tugging it over his head.

My eyes widened.

"Wait—what are you doing?" I asked, keeping steady eye contact with his face.

He shrugged innocently. "Undressing so I can take a shower."

"Do that in the bathroom," I argued as he worked on the belt of his baseball pants. My breath caught in my throat at the knowledge that if he pushed the subject, I'd be a total goner. I could see the dip of his torso, the hard lines of his abs, and suddenly I didn't want to fight against us. I stepped forward and hauled my body against him so that he had to catch me against the door. It rattled in its hinges as I wrapped my hands around his neck.

He laughed into my mouth as we kissed, completely mad for each other. His hands tugged my shirt up and I laughed as it got caught on my head for a few seconds.

"Good, just stay like that," Chase joked, not helping me tug it off.

"Hey! Help me!"

"But, I'm really enjoying the view," he quipped, skimming his hands down the center of my stomach. My muscles quivered beneath his touch even as the t-shirt started to cut off circulation.

He reached up to help pull it off, but the ominous sound of the front door opening stopped us dead in our tracks.

"Guys! I'm home. Do you want to go grab dinner?" my dad shouted up the stairs.

Chase and I scrambled apart and I yanked my t-shirt back down over my chest. In a flash of silent shouts and rushed gestures, Chase had his shirt in hand and was creeping across the hall to his room.

"Guys?"

"Okay Dad! Just one second!" I yelled back, keeping my eyes on Chase.

He turned to close his door and his wickedly handsome smile was the last thing I saw.

It was the first time I'd let my love for Chase see the light of day.

CHAPTER FIFTY-ONE

Lilah

THE FOLLOWING WEEK passed in slow motion. Each day blurred from moment to moment: walking to school, sitting through classes, pretending to be okay, avoiding questions, and putting on a fake smile for Chase. I thought that my feelings for him would settle into something comfortable, but Chase and I had passed the point of no return. I was blind with love for him and the more I realized it, the more it scared me.

I loved Chase. I loved him and no one could see how beautifully pure the feeling was. They were too consumed by the juxtaposition of what "was" and what "should be". To them, I wasn't even worthy of being a star-crossed Capulet to his Montague—I was more the serving wench that must have slipped a love potion into Romeo's stew. I'd stolen him right out from beneath Juliet.

Every day during lunch, I walked by the cafeteria and paused to take in Chase among his friends. I was like an anthropologist studying the habits of a culture I'd never been a part of. I evaded Chase's invitations to join him, choosing instead to hide out in the library or the nature center, whichever one suited my fancy that day.

It felt good to breathe on my own again, to spend thirty minutes without the constant feeling of having someone watching me, studying me, judging me.

I was standing at the door of the cafeteria on Friday when Kimberly walked by with a group of Diamond Girls. When she saw me, she waved off her friends and hung back to talk to me.

"Hey, what are you doing out here?" she asked with a friendly smile.

"Just...regrouping," I said, speaking the truth for the first time in a week.

Kimberly's eyebrows knit together. "Are you and Chase okay?"

I looked past her shoulder to see Chase reach down for a handful of fries. He was wearing his trademark smirk and I just couldn't do it any more. I couldn't fake it.

"Do you ever think about being with Chase?" I asked, ignoring her prior question altogether.

She tilted her head, her friendly smile slipping ever so slightly. "What do you mean? We dated junior year, but that's over now."

I shook my head. "No, I know that. I mean in the future."

Her eyes narrowed and she pulled her bottom lip between her teeth while she thought.

"I guess I've thought about it a little."

I took a deep breath, trying to shove aside the feeling of acid eating away at my stomach. "It's just that ever since I started dating him, I've sort of felt like an impostor." I paused, wondering if I should keep going. "And then I see you and him together and it just fits. It makes so much sense."

She smiled, obviously uncomfortable with my honesty. "But you're with him. He wants to be with you, Lilah." She pointed to my chest as if to emphasize that point.

I nodded because for now, she was right. For now, I had the golden boy, but it wouldn't last; he'd picked the wrong girl.

I swallowed down the thought, shoving it so far beneath the surface that by the time physics rolled around, I could offer Chase my best attempt at a genuine smile. Mr. Jenkins passed out the problem set and I focused on it like my life depended on it. Chase and I worked through it together while Connor lagged behind. In a lot of ways, it was the same Friday afternoon I'd had for the last few months, until Chase's phone buzzed and I glanced down to see an incoming call from Kimberly.

My stomach clenched at the sight of her name. *Did she call him often?* She was his Diamond Girl, of course she did.

I pretended not to notice the call and he ignored it, but just as we turned in our problem sets, his phone buzzed again. This time he asked to use the restroom so he could answer it. The final bell rang and he never came back.

I watched the other kids in my class bolt, including Connor, but I waited. I glanced back and forth from Chase's backpack to the door, wondering if he was going to bother coming back for it. Mr. Jenkins packed up his classroom and offered me an expectant glare.

"It looks like Chase skipped out of class early. When you see him please let him know that he'll be serving detention for that next week."

I nodded and carried out both of our backpacks, one on each shoulder.

The sky had been dark and cloudy during lunch, but the rain waited long enough for me to eat my sandwich out in the nature center. As I walked out after the final bell, I knew I wouldn't be so lucky for my walk home.

The wind whipped my hair across my face and I stared up to see dark rumbling clouds overtaking the sky. I smiled thinking about how much my plants needed the rain. It was the first time I'd smiled all week and it slipped away as soon as I looked down to see Chase walking side by side with Kimberly. He'd been running late, and now I knew why. He wasn't planning on meeting me at all.

The two of them bee-lined for her car in the parking lot. I stood frozen as she reached up to give him a hug before rounding the car toward the driver's side. My stomach twisted into a knot I was helpless to untangle. I blinked, trying to clear away the scene as they pulled out of the parking lot, wondering if my mind was playing a trick on me. Chase was leaving school with Kimberly. Why? Why would he do that? Had Kimberly told him what I'd said earlier?

My mother always told me to be careful what I wished for, and in that moment I realized how truthful her words were. I should have been more careful about airing my doubts. The universe had listened and acted much faster than I'd even thought possible.

I didn't have the golden boy any more.

A clap of thunder jostled me back to the present and I knew I needed to get a move on if I wanted to make it home before the rain started. I reached around to pull my phone out of the front pocket of my backpack and felt betrayal melt through me. There wasn't a missed call or a text message waiting to be read. The blank screen sealed my fate: Chase had left school with Kimberly and I would be walking home alone. I tucked my phone back into the front pocket of my backpack and turned to start my walk home as the first few raindrops started to fall like splatters of paint on the sidewalk.

Just perfect.

By the time I reached the front gate of the school, the rain was pouring harder than it had in years. The school's buses had already left or I would have turned around and hopped on one. My dad was still working and I didn't want to bother him. My only choice was to continue walking.

I headed around the perimeter of the school with two backpacks weighing down my body and the idea of Chase and Kimberly together weighing down my mind.

I didn't stop walking until I reached an old oak tree on Main Street. Its canopy was wide and hung low over the sidewalk. I huddled beneath it, hoping the storm would pass quickly. My clothes were soaked and each backpack had gained at least ten pounds of water weight. I dropped them to the dry ground beneath the tree and rolled my shoulders back to loosen the tension in them. The rain didn't look like it would be letting up any time soon; I knew I'd have to just suck it up until I got home.

I checked my phone again, desperate for a text from Chase, but there was nothing. I bent down to retrieve the backpacks with a groan just as a familiar silver Camry pulled to a stop against the curb right in front of me. Behind the rain-splattered windows, I watched as Trent leaned over and turned the manual crank on the window.

I pushed my wet hair behind my ear and leaned down.

"What are you doing walking home in this?" he asked with a frown.

I looked from left to right, trying to think of a good excuse. I didn't have one.

"It's not that bad. I'm almost halfway," I answered limply.

"Do you want a ride? It's not going to let up any time soon."

I looked past his car to the sidewalk covered in puddles and the rain hammering down around me. Truthfully, I'd never been so relieved to have a ride home in my life. I pulled open his passenger-side door and slid onto the seat. He reached over to shove aside a few CDs and crumpled receipts. His hand brushed my thigh and his eyes flew to mine.

"Sorry, I wasn't expecting passengers," he said with a boyish smile that wasn't something I was used to seeing on him. His black hair was cropped shorter than I'd seen, making his handsome features far easier to discern. I fidgeted in my seat, placed the backpacks between my legs, and reached over to grab my seatbelt.

"Thanks for picking me up," I said, surprised by the vulnerability in my tone.

"No problem. I usually hang out after school but I left today to beat the rain," he gestured through the front windshield. "As you can see, I didn't do a very good job of that."

I laughed, surprised by the lightness in my chest. *This feels right. Easy.*

"Do you want to go grab something to eat?" I asked.

The question was out before I'd decided whether or not it was a good idea, but I figured eating an early dinner with

Trent beat sitting at home and wondering what Chase was doing with Kimberly.

Trent's eyebrows shot up and then he nodded once, slowly, processing my question. "Yes. Yeah, okay. I know a good place we can go."

I sighed and looked out the window, soaking in the musty scent that clung to his car's upholstery. There was a small part of me that felt at home in Trent's car. Trent didn't shine the way Chase did. No one would judge me for hanging out with him. We were on the same playing field: two misfits in a small town.

CHAPTER FIFTY-TWO

Lilah

TRENT TOOK ME to a pizza joint off Main Street that was connected to an old arcade. It was the perfect place to wait out the storm as we filled our stomachs with warm cheese pizza and played Pac-Man until our thumbs were sore. The restaurant was empty save for a burly man behind the counter whose beard reached the top of his beer gut. I didn't mind him though; he flipped a switch on a few of the arcade games so that after Trent had spent twenty dollars, we could both keep playing for free.

I hadn't realized how much time we'd spent there until Trent pulled his phone out of his back pocket and offered a change of venue.

"There's a get-together over at Blake's house. Do you remember him?" he asked. I racked my brain until I recalled a guy that had graduated from our high school a few years earlier. He'd stayed in Blackwater even after graduation and I'd heard rumors that he was one of the guys supplying Trent and his friends with drugs. I chewed on my lip, trying to decide if it'd be a better idea if I just went home. It was fun hanging out with Trent for a little while, but we weren't really friends and I didn't want to regret getting stuck at a party with him.

He pocketed his phone and then gave me an innocent smile. "How about we just go check it out and if you're bored or if you want to leave, we'll head out."

I crossed my arms and took a deep breath. I was probably overthinking things. I'd go with Trent for a little bit since he'd saved me from walking home in the rain, and then I'd go back to my life and figure out how I could possibly move on from Chase. My stomach clenched at the thought and then before I could stop it, images of him and Kimberly sprang free in my mind. I could see them walking to class hand in hand. I could see her in the stands watching him play baseball with his last name on the back of her shirt. I could see him sitting down for dinner with her family, a perfect group of four.

I let Trent lead me out to his car, but I didn't pay much attention as he drove toward the outskirts of Blackwater. The roads were a muddy mess from the storm and as we pulled off in front of a doublewide trailer, I feared Trent wouldn't be able to get his car back out of the mud when it was time for us to leave.

"Ready to go in?" he asked with a cheerful tone.

I swung my door open and tried to step around most of the big piles of mud on the way to the front door. Trent went ahead of me and mapped out a safe route, but it was no use. By the time we reached the front door, my shoes were covered in mud. I tried to kick some of it off when the trailer's door swung open and two drunk girls giggled past us.

"Trent!" they called as they walked by. I smiled to myself, having forgotten the bad boy appeal most girls saw in him. He tipped his head in their direction and then put his hand on my back to guide me inside. The trailer was small and cast in a yellow glow from the old fluorescent bulbs that hung from the ceiling. A tattered, stained couch sat directly next to the door and there were three boys each rolling a joint, trying to race one another to completion. I looked past them toward the kitchen and saw Ashley chatting with Blake.

It wasn't until I saw her that I realized how underdressed I was for the occasion. I hadn't bothered to put much makeup on before school and I was still wearing jeans and an old Rolling Stones t-shirt.

Ashley was decked out in a short denim skirt and a white lacy tank top. Her four-inch heels added to her height and when Blake straightened up after pouring her a drink, she towered over him.

He was just as I suspected: a guy in his late twenties with a slight beer belly and thick, gelled black hair. In other words, he looked like someone who shouldn't have been partying with a bunch of high schoolers. As I stood, taking him in, Ashley looked up and spotted me. I braced myself for an awkward encounter, but her shock was quickly replaced with a giant smile.

"Lilah!" she squealed, stumbling in her high heels to reach me.

I laughed and reached out to help stabilize her as she all but fell onto me. "Hi Ashley."

"I can't believe you're here! How did Trent talk you into

coming? I thought you only hung out with Chase now."

I rolled my eyes and released her arms.

"I hang out with whoever I want to, and tonight I'm here to see you," I said, putting on a fake smile.

Trent tapped my arm and motioned toward the kitchen where Blake was still standing, watching my encounter with Ashley. I wondered if I'd interrupted something between the two of them.

"I'll go get us some drinks, be right back," Trent said.

Ashley took the opportunity and tugged me toward the couch. The guys moved over for us and I let Ashley squeeze in next to them so I could sit on the arm of the couch.

Ashley took a joint from one of the guys and took a hit. She offered it to me but I held up my hand in protest.

"Here you go," Trent said, appearing by my side with a red Solo cup in hand. He grinned wide as I took the cup and peered inside.

"What is this?" I asked, taking a sniff. There was a faint hint of alcohol but it wasn't too overwhelming.

"A rum and Coke. I went easy on the rum because I knew you'd give me hell," he joked, bending down to take a seat on the edge of the couch.

I smiled and took a tentative first sip, relieved to find that it was mostly coke.

"Let's play King's Cup!" Ashley said, clapping her hands together with glee.

Blake pulled open a kitchen drawer to retrieve a tattered deck of cards and then tossed them over to us. Trent caught them midair, pulled open the box, and started to shuffle the cards on his lap.

Ashley brushed me up on the rules of the game as I finished my first drink. Trent stood to get me another one, but I held up my hand to stop him. I wanted the first one to settle in before I had any more. It hadn't tasted very strong, but I didn't want the rum to hit me all at once.

"I'll just fill it with water. You need a drink to play the game," Trent whispered in my ear. I smiled and blinked, feeling a faint lightness in my head, probably from the smoke in the air. Water was a good idea.

When he returned, I took a few sips as people started drawing cards.

Ashley reached forward and picked up a two of hearts. "Two, you!" she said, turning and pointing to me.

"What does that mean?" I asked, trying to recall the rules she'd just explained. My head felt fuzzy and I tried to blink away the confusion.

"When someone draws a two, they get to point to whoever they want and that person has to take a drink with them. So drink up!" she hollered into my ear.

I gulped down some of the water, but as I pulled the cup away from my mouth the room spun around me.

"Trent are you sure there wasn't much rum in that drink?" I asked, looking up at him. The edges of his face were blurred and I squinted, trying to make him out in the fuzziness.

He smiled and shrugged. "Nope. Not much rum at all."

I should have paid more attention to that grin, but it was my turn to draw a card. I reached out to grab a card off the top of the deck and everyone shouted. I blinked my eyes again, feeling the same dizziness overtaking me. When I moved to sit back in my seat, a sharp feeling of vertigo overtook over me.

I tried to tell Ashley that I had a headache and didn't want to keep playing, but the words came out muddled and slow.

"What the hell did you put in her drink, Trent?" Ashley snapped.

The last thing I remembered was the laughter of the three boys rolling joints on the couch. They sounded like a pack of cackling hyenas.

CHAPTER FIFTY-THREE

Chase

SPRINGTIME HAD ALWAYS let me down. The season had an uncanny ability to disappoint me and that year was no different, except for Lilah. That year I had Lilah. Lilah and a drunk dad.

Kimberly had called me twice during Physics and by the time I'd finally returned her call in the guys bathroom, she was frantic.

"Your dad was in an accident."

"What?"

"A car accident," she clarified.

I stared at myself in the bathroom mirror and asked the question that could forever change my life.

"Is he still alive?"

The details were minimal: my dad had been driving home when he'd run his car off the road. An ambulance had taken him to the county hospital where Kimberly's mom, an ER nurse, had been there to admit him.

I met Kimberly at the back of the school and followed her out to her car, hoping she'd have a lead foot the entire drive to the hospital. I couldn't think past the idea of being an orphan, of being completely alone. *Can someone become an orphan at eighteen or is that a term only used for children?* My dad was hardly a dad, but he was better than nothing.

Kimberly put her car into park and I ran inside the emergency waiting room, scrambling to find someone who could point me in the right direction. There were bright-colored signs everywhere, leading to and from wards and check-in desks.

I ran to the first desk I saw and tried to speak as calmly as possible.

"Excuse me," I said to the nurse. She was multitasking, filling out a chart while on the phone. I didn't care. "Excuse me."

"Just give me a second," she said, eyeing me with annoyance.

There was a spectrum between the two possibilities and I didn't know which end of it I should start preparing for. If I prepared myself for the worst, then I couldn't be surprised.

The set of double doors beside the reception desk swung open and Kimberly's mom stepped into the waiting room in pale blue scrubs. Without a word, she guided me back to sit in a chair against the wall. Her kind eyes sought mine and she took a deep breath before beginning.

"I don't want to sugarcoat this for you, Chase. Your

father was in a very bad accident. His car flipped off the road and landed upside down in a ditch. The paramedics were called to the scene immediately and the fire department helped pull him from the car. Once they had him in the ambulance, they checked his blood alcohol level. Most people would have been unconscious with the amount of alcohol he had in his system."

"He's built up a high tolerance over the years," I explained, not to defend him, but just to explain that sad fact to her.

She blinked and kept her eyes closed for a moment before continuing.

"There's quite a bit of internal bleeding. He's in surgery now so the doctors can find the source and repair the damage as best as possible. Once they have that under control they can focus on the other injuries he sustained."

"Did he hurt anyone else on the road?" I asked, needing to know that answer before continuing. I couldn't care about my father's injuries until I knew if he'd injured anyone else.

"Thankfully, no."

I took a deep breath and then sat there listening to her continue to list the damage. It was surprisingly hard to hear it all through unbiased ears. My mind was already spinning scenarios, trying to figure out how it would impact my father. Would he care? Would he change his life? Would he go right back to his self-destructive ways?

I felt sick at how impossibly selfish he'd been getting behind the wheel of car in that kind of state, even worse so because I knew it hadn't been the first time. I had never felt more grateful for Gough Galloway's foresight in taking me in; this was exactly the kind of thing he wanted to protect me from.

Mrs. White patted my hand and promised to update me as soon as she had more information. I nodded and let her walk back through the shiny chrome double doors.

I'm not sure how long I sat there before Kimberly walked in with some Chinese food from a restaurant down the street. I guessed she'd gone to grab something after dropping me off.

"Here, you should eat," she said, opening the to-go boxes and preparing a small meal for me. The thought of food repulsed me, but I didn't want to offend her, so I took the plate and set it on my lap, swirling the noodles into a smooth spiral.

I wanted Lilah to be there. I wanted her to tell me everything would be all right, and even if it wasn't all right, I wanted her to be there so I'd know that at the end of the day I still had the one person I cared about, the only person that truly mattered.

I reached down for my phone in my pocket, but didn't feel it.

"I think I left my phone in your car," I said, already moving to stand with my plate of food.

"No. Stay, I'll go grab it."

Lilah was probably wondering why I hadn't met up with her after school, but gossip spread like wildfire in our town and hopefully someone thought to notify her. Still, when Kimberly handed me my phone, I dialed her number from memory and waited through the rings so I could tell her to come down to the hospital myself. When her voicemail picked up, I hung up and tried calling her again.

"I'm sure she's eating dinner or something," Kimberly said, trying to exude positive energy. My gut knew better. My gut needed Lilah to answer her phone.

• • •

By the time my dad's surgeon called me back from the waiting room, I still hadn't heard from Lilah. I pocketed my phone and pushed past the swinging doors. Dr. Williams was in charge of my father's care and I was surprised by how young he looked.

I tried to keep up as he explained how well the surgery had gone, how likely it was that my father would have a full recovery. They'd gotten the internal bleeding under control and they were going to reset the bones in his forearm and wrist. He had a punctured lung and a few gashes that needed stitches, but Dr. Williams explained that he'd be able to leave the hospital in a few days.

"Is it just you and your father at the house?" he asked, trying to get a feel for who might be handling my father's care.

"Yes, just us," I answered, leaving out the fact that I hadn't been living with him for the past few months.

"All right. We'll get him set up with a homecare nurse, but you'll be an important part of his recovery over the next few weeks. He won't need you as much once he's off the medications, but the first few days will be a little rocky."

I nodded, recalling all the times throughout high school I'd taken care of him after he'd drunk himself sick. Caring for him after surgery would be no different, really. Dr. Williams started walking down the hallway and instructed me to follow after him. We reached another set of double doors and he scanned his ID and ushered me into the critical care unit.

Nurses were rushing to and from rooms with metal clipboards in hand and bleak expressions covering their faces. We kept walking deeper down the hallway until we stopped outside room 178. I stood in front of the glossy wooden door willing myself to go inside.

"You can go on in, but he'll probably be sleeping," Dr. Williams said, patting me on the shoulder. "His nurse will come in soon and discuss the recovery plan with you so everyone is on the same page."

I nodded and gripped the door handle. *Time to face the music.* The hospital smell that had lingered faintly in the hallway hit me full force as I walked into my dad's room. The sterile chemicals practically burned my lungs.

My dad was lying in a tangle of cords, IVs, and monitors. His face was covered in bruises and scratches. What parts I could see were stark white. I hadn't realized how thin he'd become in the recent months, but his sunken cheekbones emphasized the bruising around his eyes and nose even more. His right arm was hoisted in a sling mounted to a pole over his head, and the left side of his robe protruded out from the padding they'd wrapped around his lungs.

I wasn't sure how long I stood there on the other side of his bed in a catatonic state. Nurses flitted in and out of the room, checking whatever they thought needed checking and leaving me alone for the most part. I think they knew I didn't feel like talking and maybe they were relieved by that. They could do their job in peace and then move on to the next patient.

Sometime later, they woke him up while I stayed rooted to the same spot. The orthopedist needed him awake while he reset his arm. He was groggy when the nurse woke him up and I couldn't understand most of what slipped out of his mouth. It was the ramblings of a lunatic as far as I was concerned.

When he could focus long enough to see me standing at the foot of his bed, he swallowed slowly and then glanced away, unable to meet my eyes for long.

Pathetic.

I watched the orthopedist reset his bones and then wrap his arm tightly in gauze and an elastic bandage before fitting it back into the sling. My father winced and moaned the entire time. I was sure it was incredibly painful, but I didn't have much sympathy for him.

When they were done, the medical staff left the room and the heart monitor was the only thing disturbing the ominous silence hanging between us.

He spoke first. "I don't want to hear it."

His ambivalence pissed me off even more and I narrowed my eyes on him. "You're such an asshole."

The layer of respect that's supposed to underpin a father-son relationship no longer existed for us. He was a pathetic excuse for what a father should have been and I was so angry with him I couldn't control it any longer.

"Watch your mouth. You think you can disrespect me now that you're eighteen and going off to some fancy college?"

I rolled my eyes at his empty words. He was currently constrained to a hospital bed, probably still half-drunk. Respect wasn't even an option any more.

I was about to open my mouth again when I felt a vibration in my back pocket. I looked down and saw Lilah's name across the screen; my heart sank. *Finally.* I left my father's room and stepped out into the hallway to answer the call.

"Lilah? I need you to come down to the hospital."

"Chase. Chase? This is Ashley. She sounded like she was inside a tunnel; I could hardly hear her.

"Ashley? What? Speak up."

"Chase. Can you hear me? Lilah needs your help."

Those four words were enough to bring me to my knees.

"What? Where is she?" I tugged my hand through my hair, already heading toward the entrance of the hospital.

"We're at Blake Vaughn's house and I think one of the guys put something in her drink."

My heart hammered in my chest as I tried to process her words.

Blake Vaughn.

Blake the big time dealer.

I rushed through the hospital doors and ran out into the parking lot, only to realize that I didn't have my truck. *Fuck.* I was helpless. It was at least two miles from the hospital to Lilah's house. I shouted at Ashley to text me Blake's address, pocketed my phone, and took off in a dead sprint.

CHAPTER FIFTY-FOUR

Chase

THOSE TWO MILES were endless. My feet pounded the pavement, my heart hammered in my chest, my breath echoed in my ears, and my legs stung with exhaustion. I rounded the corner to Lilah's house and saw Mr. Calloway's car sitting in the driveway. Harvey barked behind the front door, but I didn't have a minute to spare. I hopped in my truck, slammed the door, and gunned it out of the driveway.

I plugged Blake's address into my phone as I sped away from downtown. During the drive I tried to calm my racing heart by repeating the same phrase over and over. *She's okay. She's okay.* I shoved my hand through my hair, tugging the ends, and trying to figure out how shit could hit the fan so quickly and completely.

The map lead me down a road with tire tracks leading

through mud. I pushed my foot down on the gas and passed a grouping of trees. Heavy bass was the first clue that I was getting closer to the party and then I finally saw a doublewide trailer surrounded by cars. My eyes locked onto Trent's silver Camry and my hands squeezed the steering wheel so hard I thought I'd rip it right out of the dashboard.

I swung my truck behind the parked cars and hopped out into the mud. I couldn't think beyond getting inside and finding Lilah. I didn't bother knocking on the cheap door. I pushed it open with my shoulder and broke it off one of the hinges.

The smell of marijuana and cigarette smoke mingled in the air as my eyes darted around the small space, trying to find Lilah's short black hair. There was a group of guys sitting on the couch, too high to care what was going on around them. I looked past them, into the kitchen, to find Ashley shouting at a guy that I vaguely recognized. Blake. I charged forward just as Ashley tried to get past him. He wrapped his hand around her arm and pushed her back against the counter. She yelped as his grip tightened around her arm.

"What the hell are you doing?" I yelled, throwing myself between them. Blake hadn't noticed me until that moment. His eyes widened and then narrowed accusingly as he dropped Ashley's arm.

"Who let you in? This is a private party, asshole," Blake spat out, stepping closer and sizing me up. I was smack-dab in the middle of the hardest day of my life. I could have easily taken my anger out on his face.

"Chase, get Lilah!" Ashley said, tugging on the back of my shirt to get my attention.

I shoved past Blake in pursuit of the closed door at the

end of the hallway. He shouted after me, but I didn't listen. I could see light streaming through the bottom, but when I tried the knob, it was locked. I reared back and threw myself against the door. It sprang open and I stumbled inside the room, catching my momentum as Trent jumped from the bed.

"Bro, this isn't what you think," he said, holding his hands up in innocence.

His words meant nothing; I was already in a blind rage as I caught sight of Lilah flat on the bed. Her head was lolled to the side. Her short black hair covered half of her face. Her eyes were closed, her cheeks were pale, and her clothes were still on.

"I was trying to take care of her," he offered lamely.

I rounded the bed and leaned over to check her breathing. Her breaths were shallow and slow. I was about to scoop her up into my arms when Trent's movement caught my attention.

He was trying to leave.

Maybe on a better day, I would have let him go. Maybe on a better day, he could have escaped. But it wasn't a better day.

I reached for the back of his shirt and threw him against the wall of the trailer. His head hit the cheap wood paneling and a few shelves clattered to the floor along with all of the cheap shit piled on top of them. I didn't give him time to recover; I walked over and pulled him up off the ground with the collar of his shirt.

"Do you think this is fucking game? Do you think you can play with people's lives like this?" I asked, fighting my grip around his throat.

His gaze darted back and forth between my eyes. His hands scraped at my fist, but I was working off too much adrenaline and rage to notice the sting.

"Listen, man," he pleaded. "We were just having fun. I didn't know she..." His voice was starting to crack. He had been about to rape my girlfriend and he thought he deserved pity. I tightened my grip around his neck and his eyes widened in fear. I couldn't see past my anger. Red rage clouded my vision as Trent struggled for air.

I would have killed him. Had I walked in five minutes later and Lilah's shirt been on the ground or her pants unbuttoned, I would have destroyed him.

I heard commotion in the kitchen and I knew I only had a few seconds before Blake came in to help out his friend. I looked Trent straight in the eye and then tossed him to the ground. He crumbled to a heap and clutched his legs into the fetal position. He was prepared for more abuse, but it wasn't coming.

I needed to get Lilah out of the trailer before things got worse.

Blake was yelling in the kitchen as I reached down to scoop her up off the bed. She stirred in my arms, blinking her eyes open just barely.

"I was just dreaming of you," she whispered, rolling her head toward my chest and inhaling.

"Are you my angel?" she asked with a small smile. "You smell like one."

My heart broke.

"Lilah, can you hear me?" I asked, trying to keep her awake and cognizant.

"Silly, silly, silly. Your mom tried to be my mom's angel, but she didn't know she'd get her wish." She tapped her finger against my chest in time with her words. "I don't want you to end up an angel," she crooned, nestling against my chest and continuing to mumble. "I can't be saved. We can't be saved. Don't you see that?"

She was laughing, a soft, quiet laugh that turned dark. Suddenly, her smile contorted and she squeezed her eyes closed as she started to cry.

"I'll only hurt you. "

"You can't hurt me," I argued, though I knew it was pointless. She wouldn't remember any of this in the morning.

"I already have," she slurred.

I glanced up to see Blake standing in the doorway gripping a long kitchen knife. Sweat collected on his brow and he fidgeted on his feet, nervous despite the fact that he was the one wielding a weapon.

"Get out of my house," he yelled, pointing the knife out toward me. "NOW!"

I should have been nervous. He was a maniac with a knife, but with Lilah in my arms, there was no room for fear.

I stepped toward him and he stepped back. I knew he wouldn't use the knife. He was holding it out like he was going to do something with it, but he was scared. The blade bobbled back and forth in his shaky hand. He backed up into the kitchen, careful not to stumble over his feet. Everyone was gone.

"Where's Ashley?" I asked.

"She gone. I kicked 'em out," Blake answered gruffly. I'd have to take his word for it. I needed to get Lilah out of there.

He backed up to the kitchen counter and trailed my every move with his knife. The blade was only a foot away from me; he could have reached out and used it, but he backed up and ran for the bedroom to help Trent.

I kicked the front door open and walked out into the

quiet woods without glancing back. Had Blake been a little bolder, maybe he would have thought seriously about using that knife, but when it came down to it, guys like him were cowards. Drugging girls to take advantage of them was a testament to that.

I held Lilah up with my knee while I opened the door to my truck. Once she was lying across the bench seat, I rounded the front, slid inside, and propped her head up on my lap.

After her slurred speech in Blake's trailer, she'd drifted off. I couldn't tell if she was sleeping or passed out, but I made sure to keep checking her pulse as I drove the few miles back to the hospital.

I carried her into the emergency room and did my best to ignore everyone's stares. I could only imagine how bad we looked. I was carrying my girlfriend in my arms, she was unconscious, and I was covered in mud and sweat.

I walked up to the nurse sitting behind the glass window, relieved to find that she wasn't the one I'd dealt with earlier. As soon as she saw Lilah in my arms, she hopped up and buzzed the swinging doors so I could step back into the hallway. She pulled out a rolling bed from a spare room and I laid Lilah on top of it as I began to explain the situation as best I could.

"My girlfriend was drugged at a party. I don't know what they gave her, but her breathing has been inconsistent since I got to her. She was awake and talking for a second, but she hasn't said anything in a while."

The nurse nodded and started wheeling Lilah down the hallway. I moved to follow after her but a police officer stepped up and blocked my path. I tried to look past him to figure out where they were taking Lilah, but his burly shoulders made it impossible to see around him.

"Would you mind coming with me for a moment, son?" His dark eyes stared down at me and I knew he thought I'd had something to do with the drugs.

Despite my protests, the police officer led me to a conference room down the hall. It was small, with a simple round table and six plastic chairs positioned around it. A white dry-erase board took up one entire wall and there was still writing on it from a previous meeting, a bunch of medical jargon I didn't understand.

"Take a seat," he instructed.

I had to fight to control my temper. I'd just lived through six hours of hell and now I was about to get interrogated by an officer. It was complete bullshit.

"So you brought your friend in after she'd been drugged. Were you two at a party?" he asked, leaning forward to rest his hands on the top of the table.

I sighed and started from the beginning. I described my afternoon: rushing to the hospital to take care of my father who was still in room 178, probably passed out from the morphine they were giving him for the pain. I told him about Ashley's phone call, described Blake as best as I could, and gave the officer his address. Somewhere in the middle of my explanation his brows relaxed and he took a seat across from me, dropping the tough guy act altogether.

He believed me because there was no reason not to. My explanation added up and he revealed that Blake already had a criminal history a mile long.

"Thank you for cooperating," he said, pushing back his chair. "Just had to follow protocol."

I nodded and shoved my hands through my hair. I was tired down to my bones. My brain was fried and my limbs felt heavy. I could have passed out in my seat, but Lilah still needed me. I was at a total loss for where to go. The police officer didn't know where they'd taken Lilah, so I had to hunt down a nurse to help me find her. Before I went into her room, I went into the men's room and splashed water on my face, trying to regroup and collect my scattered nerves. I could still picture her on Blake's bed, ghostly pale. I'd been so close to losing her and my nerves were still frayed.

I took a deep breath before opening her door. She was lying on the same kind of sterile bed my dad was still occupying on the other side of the hospital. Her dark hair was matted with sweat around her temples and her lips were dry and chapped. I walked to the side of her bed and reached down for her small hand, closing my fist around it. I stared down at the connection between us and let the last hour sink into my bones. The first tears that came were surprising and I wiped them away quickly. The ones that came after were heavy and sad. I bent down and rested my head on the side of her bed, completely exhausted.

The nurses came in and I stared at Lilah's soft features as they assured me she'd be fine, that her dad was already there talking with the doctors. Trent had put Rohypnol in her drink, but by the morning she'd be good as new. No signs of abuse, no lasting damage. All was well.

Mrs. White brought me a cot and a gray wool blanket. The cot fit in the space between Lilah's bed and the wall so it was easy to settle in next to her and watch her chest rise and fall as she slept. I reached back out to hold her hand, wrapping my palm around her cold fingers. She never stirred once, but I still watched her for hours, trying to read her calm features for signs of the lost girl that lived inside.

CHAPTER FIFTY-FIVE

Lilah

I **WOKE UP** Saturday morning with a splitting headache and a gaping void where memories of the night before should have been. I blinked open my eyes and stared up at a pristine white ceiling divided into eight panels. I adjusted on the bed and felt the IV needle in the back of my hand and the unfamiliar scratchy bedding. My mind was still foggy until I saw the hospital gown and Chase sleeping soundly in the cot beside my bed.

I remembered being with Trent at the arcade. I remembered him driving us to a party at one of his friend's houses, and I remembered seeing Ashley there, but there was nothing beyond that. I couldn't figure out how I'd landed in the hospital or why Chase was laying there beside me. The last time I'd seen him he'd been hopping into Kimberly's car.

The door to my hospital room slid open and a young nurse with a bright smile and tired eyes sauntered in to check the machines beeping methodically next to my bed. She fidgeted with a few cords and then reached down to adjust something beside my bed.

"How are you feeling?" she asked, keeping her voice low so she wouldn't wake Chase.

"Fine, I guess, but I'm not sure why I'm here." My words scraped against my sandpaper throat.

I wiggled my fingers and toes and then lifted up the neck of my gown to look down at my chest. There wasn't a scratch on me.

"Last night you were given a drink with Rohypnol in it while you were at a party," the nurse explained before pointing at Chase. "That boy right there found you and brought you in here to make sure you were okay."

I looked at Chase's sleeping features as the pieces of my memory started to slowly reform: Trent getting me a drink, feeling dizzy after I took a few sips, and then nothing.

I focused on the curve of his cheekbones as I asked the next question.

"I wasn't, um…" I looked down at the bed sheet. "No one took advantage of me, did they?"

The side of her mouth tilted up. "No. Seems that your hero has good timing. I think the police have already brought the two men from the party in for questioning though."

She checked one last thing on my vitals and then headed back for the door.

"The doctor will be in to talk to you soon, but you should be cleared to head home today. The drugs are all out of your system now," she said.

"Okay. Thank you."

The noise of her closing the door jarred Chase from his final remnants of sleep. He turned on the cot, blinked his eyes open toward the ceiling, and then glanced toward me.

"Hi," I said, suddenly feeling vulnerable.

He groaned as he sat up in the cot and then stretched his arms overhead, undoubtedly sore from his makeshift bed.

"How are you feeling?" he asked in a sleepy tone.

"I'm good. Thank you for coming to get me last night. How did you know I was there?"

He grunted. "Ashley called me after Trent pushed you into the bedroom."

The audible sound of my heart rate picking up served as an indicator of how pissed I was at the mention of Trent.

"Why were you even with those guys?" Chase asked.

I took my time trying to think of a good reason, but when I couldn't, I shrugged and looked him dead in the eye. "Trent gave me a ride when I was walking home in the rain. He invited me to the party and I decided to go for a little bit. It was a better plan than sitting at home by myself."

Chase's eyebrows tugged together in confusion. "Are you angry?"

I shrugged, remembering how easily he'd left me behind to get in the car with Kimberly.

"Don't you know what happened?"

His earnest expression made my shoulders sag. "No. What are you talking about?"

He pinched the bridge of his nose and then explained in shorthand what he'd gone through the day before: the car accident, Kimberly telling him at school. The scene in the parking lot made perfect sense, but I'd seen what my insecurities had wanted me to see.

"I thought you were ditching me for Kimberly," I admitted with an embarrassed whisper. How could I have been so self-centered? How could I have had so little trust in him? Maybe in my obsession, I had started to see secrets where there were none.

He pushed off his cot and moved to sit on the edge of my bed, just against my left leg.

"You honestly thought I'd do that? We're dating Lilah. I love you."

I squeezed my eyes closed and wished I could tell him how much I loved him too, but I was drowning. Even though his words soothed my insecurities, they also stoked fiery feelings of self-loathing. What if Trent had taken advantage of me the night before? I'd been stupid enough to put myself in that situation in the first place.

Before I could open my mouth, the hospital door slid open and my dad stepped into the room. He let out a visible sigh when he saw me sitting up and then tilted his head toward the door.

"Chase, do you mind if I have a talk with Lilah for a second?" my dad asked.

Chase pushed up off the cot but didn't bother looking back at me as he exited the room. When the door clicked back into place, my dad sighed and wiped his palms down his cheeks, giving me an exasperated look.

"You can't do that to me, kid," he began. "I tried calling you two dozen times last night and when you didn't answer. Do you know how scared I was, trying to figure out where you'd gone? Chase's dad was in an accident and you were lost..." His voice shrank to a whisper. "It brought back memories of...that day."

I opened my mouth to apologize but he kept going.

"You're grounded for the rest of the school year."

I nodded.

"There's less than a month left before you graduate, and that means you have one month left to get your head screwed on right." He paused and took a seat on the end of my bed. "I know you've had it harder than any of us after your mother died. It's not fair, but you are going to have to learn sooner than anybody else your age that just because a bad thing has happened, it doesn't mean the world is going to stop hitting you. Just look at Chase's dad."

"I'm not going to—"

"I've tried to be there for you, but there are just some things that a father can't do."

I felt tears collecting at the corner of my eyes. "Dad, you've done everything you could. You've been a good fath—"

He held up his hand to cut me off. "I know, I know. You don't have to tell me that. I want you to go college as the confident woman that I know you to be. I'm not a fool. I know that you and Chase have been seeing each other, but I trusted you two to make smart decisions. I had a tough choice to make with that: either I kicked him out and he'd be forced to move back in with his father, or I could dig my heels in and hope that maybe he'd be able to help you work through some of the grief you've kept buried inside."

I shook my head. "I don't have grief buried inside," I argued.

He tilted his head, narrowing his eyes to study me. "Your mom was fighting her own demons. Her death had nothing to do with you."

His blunt words caught me by surprise and I inhaled a sharp breath. He'd never talked about her death like that before.

"Some people slay their demons. Not everyone kills themselves," I argued.

His frown deepened. "Maybe hers were a little bit bigger than other people's."

"Yeah?" I leaned forward and pointed at my chest. "Well, what does it say about her love for us if it didn't outweigh the demons?"

"Is that what you think? That she didn't love you enough?" He reached his hand out to rest it on the blanket covering my legs. Tears slipped down my cheeks and I was helpless to stop them.

"She loved you, Lilah."

I wasn't ready to process his words; my grief was still covered in dust and decay.

The doctor came in later that morning and gave me the green light to go home. I changed into normal clothes while my dad gathered my things. When we had everything packed up, I followed my dad out of the room to find Chase waiting outside, leaning against the wall with his feet crossed and his head tilted down. I wondered what he was staring at, but I didn't get to ask before he glanced up.

"Did you go check on your dad?" I asked.

He nodded and crossed his arms as my dad headed for the elevators, giving us a moment to talk alone.

"Is he doing better? You never told me how bad his injuries were," I asked.

"He's staying in the hospital for another few nights but then they'll release him to go home. They set up a nurse for home care but I'm moving back to help too."

I froze. "You're moving back to your house?"

Chase let his head fall back against the wall and he stared up at the ceiling. "The doctor said he needs someone to stay with him and I can't just leave him like that."

"No, of course not," I said. Of course Chase would take care of his dad. I just hadn't thought about the possibility of him moving out. "How long will you stay?"

"Until I leave for college."

He was dislodging my world piece by piece. No, I told myself. It doesn't have to be that bad.

"We'll still see each other at school, and I can help you take care of your dad," I said, trying to make the best of the situation.

Chase blew out a puff of air and let his gaze fall to me. I'd never seen his hazel eyes look so sad. Those eyes were the first sign of his heartbreak.

"Lilah, are you in love with me?"

I took a step back.

"What?

"Are you in love with me?" he asked again, slower this time.

I squeezed my eyes closed as a long, sad pause passed between us.

"I…"

He sighed and then laughed pitifully. "I love you." I snapped my eyes open as he continued, "I love you and you got in that car with Trent. Why would you go with him? Do you not trust me at all?"

I shook my head.

"Why won't you answer me?" He kept firing question after question. "Why does everyone I love end up leaving me? My mom, my dad, now y—"

"It doesn't matter!" I yelled, interrupting him. "Don't you see that? It's exactly why you shouldn't love me. I'm not good enough for you!" I pointed between the two of us and let the floodgates open. "You should be with someone like Kimberly. When you go to college, there will be girls throwing themselves at you left and right. You'll finally realize how much better you can do."

"Lilah, you're beautiful," he said.

I shook my head angrily. "That's not what this is about! I'm not insecure about my looks. I don't give a shit about how I look or how you look." I pointed at my chest. "I'm talking about the inside...the gritty parts." I took a breath and continued. "Underneath it all, you're perfect. You'd do anything for the people you love and that's why you're with me. You want to be my hero. I'm the sad, broken girl you grew up with, and you want to swoop in and save the day. I don't even think you realize you're doing it."

"What are you talking about?" he argued. His brows were furrowed and his eyes were clouded in confusion.

I took a step back and felt the shift...the beginning of the end.

"I never asked for a hero, Chase. I don't want to be saved."

He stood there watching me with his lips parted and his brows tugged together. He had no clue what I was talking about, but he'd figure it out one day, and when he did, he'd know that I'd been right to walk away. I didn't need him as my hero.

I kept backing away until I bumped into a nurse behind me.

"Oh, excuse me," she said, gripping my shoulder to make sure I didn't tip over. That's when the first tear fell. I dropped my head so she wouldn't see it.

"I'm sorry," I mumbled before I spun and headed for the elevator. Chase stayed frozen in place, watching me walk away.

CHAPTER FIFTY-SIX

Chase

I GRIPPED THE steering wheel of my truck and tried to work up the courage to go inside the Calloways' house and grab my things. It'd been 24 hours since Lilah had walked away from me in the hospital. I'd stood there, trying to wrap my head around her thoughts, but in the end I was no closer to understanding her.

Eventually, I'd left. I'd gone to room 178 and stayed with my dad, listening carefully as the nurses taught me about his home care. He didn't deserve my attention, but he had no one else. For the next week or two, he'd be bedbound, which meant if he wanted to eat, I had to feed him. If he had to shit, I had to help him. Really, compared to the past few years, nothing was different. He was the child, I was the parent; our roles were finally coming full circle.

The doctors promised my dad would be discharged and ready to go home in a few days, so I wanted to move my stuff back into the house, clean it up, and get settled before then. Every pack of cigarettes was going in the trash and every bottle of alcohol was going down the drain. If I was going to help nurse him back to health, he'd be sober for every excruciating second of my time there.

With that resolution, I finally pushed open the door of my truck and walked toward the Calloways' front door. I couldn't sit in their driveway all day. Lilah and I would have to face each other in school, so I might as well get the first awkward encounter over with.

I knocked gently and then walked inside, relieved to find the living room empty save for Harvey. He'd been waiting patiently for me behind the door, but he was a whining, wagging ball of energy. I bent down and let him lick my face, smiling for the first time in two days. His soft whines told me how much he'd missed me. I knew Lilah and Mr. Calloway were taking care of him for me, but it felt better to have him back. He and I were a team. Even when I didn't have my dad or Lilah, I knew I had Harvey.

"C'mon boy, let's go get my stuff."

He barked and wagged his tail, turning circles around my legs as I stood.

There were boxes piled up by the stairs, ten or twelve in total, neatly stacked with my name scribbled on the side of them. I recognized Coach Calloway's handwriting, and when I stepped closer, I saw he'd stuck a note to the box on top.

Thought I'd help you pack. I'll come by the house tomorrow and check on you and your dad. Let me know if you need anything or if you change your mind.

- Coach

I crumpled up the note and shoved it into my pocket before picking up the first box. I made quick work of transporting them all to my truck. Harvey followed me back and forth, curious about where we were going. Once I loaded up the last one, I turned to him.

"I just need to check my room," I said, bending down and rubbing behind his ear.

He was anxious to leave, but I had to make sure Coach Calloway had packed everything. I hadn't seen my cameras inside any of the boxes and I couldn't leave without them, even if I wouldn't have the time to work on them.

I took the stairs two at a time with Harvey at my feet. Lilah's door was closed, but I ignored it anyway; she wasn't coming out any time soon. I needed my cameras and she needed her space.

I pushed the door open into my room and bent down to look under the bed. I shoved the comforter aside and spotted my cameras and tools sitting there, forgotten. I pulled out the two boxes, dusted off the tops, and sat back on my heels. A quick scan around the room proved that Coach Calloway had packed up everything else. The room looked just like it had when I'd first moved in. It had never really belonged to me. It was borrowed, just like everything else in my life.

I glanced over at the stack of boxes in the corner and paused on the biggest one on the bottom. It had always held my attention more than the other boxes. It was the one I'd tried to cover with angry pen strokes, but it hadn't helped. Her name was still there beneath the ink. *Elaine.* I moved before I realized what I was doing. I deconstructed the stack and ripped the lid off that box, looking for answers in the confines of stale, moldy cardboard. I pushed aside old newspaper clippings and saved birthday cards and then my finger skimmed across the binding of an old book.

I pulled it from the box and turned it over in my hand. It was ancient and fragile. I blew off a layer of dust across the front cover and then flipped it open.

I barely made it two pages in before jumping to my feet. *Lilah*.

CHAPTER FIFTY-SEVEN

Lilah

I WAS OUT working in my garden when Chase came to get a few things from his room. I heard his truck rumble into the driveway, but I kept my gaze trained on the plants in front of me. Everything was blooming nicely. In a week's time, the green beans and squash would be ready to pick and the tomatoes would be falling off their vines. I'd already plucked some of them. They were green and could have done well with another few days on the vine, but I didn't want the squirrels to get to them first. They'd ripen up nicely inside.

I grabbed my basket of vegetables and turned toward the house just as Chase pushed the screen door open. He held his hand up to shield the sunlight and for a moment I was taken aback by the sight of him. He was golden in every sense of the word. Tan and blond and pure hearted.

"Your garden is lookin' good," he said, eyeing the beds behind me. I followed his gaze and tried to see it all from his perspective. My garden was having a good year so far. The raspberries hadn't come in yet, but everything else was doing well.

"Thanks. Let me put some of these tomatoes in a bag so you can take them to your dad," I said, walking up the back steps to the stack of folded grocery bags I kept in a basket near the back door. We both reached down for one, but he beat me to it. He whipped it open and held it out so I could drop the tomatoes inside.

When it was filled up, I folded the top down and gave him a small smile.

"You didn't really give me the chance to talk yesterday," he said.

I swallowed and shoved my hands into my back pockets, praying he wouldn't try and rehash the argument. It'd only been one day; we hadn't even given the dust time to settle.

"You and I need time apart," he said, holding my gaze.

I tilted my head and stared up at him, confused by his change of attitude.

"Not because I don't love you and not because we won't end up together. No. You see, you and me, Lilah, we're a done deal."

"Are we?"

He crossed his arms confidently. "I'd like to think so."

I glanced away, trying to get a grip on the tears before he noticed them. I didn't want to cry. We weren't fighting or breaking up or screaming; that part was done. Even still, I couldn't stop the sadness from welling up inside of me.

"But even if you don't come back to me, I think we'll

be okay," he continued.

I focused on the side of the porch, biting the inside of my cheek to keep my protests inside, but it didn't work. They spilled out anyway.

"I thought you said you wanted to give me a happy ending?"

He smiled a sad smile that never reached his eyes. "Maybe instead I have to be satisfied with a happy middle."

I shook my head, confused.

"Think about it. Does the ending even matter? Shouldn't the middle be the happy part? It's the biggest chunk of our life, and yet no one ever asks if two people had a happy middle. They care too much about the ending."

I shook my head and wiped my nose, trying to keep the sadness hidden away. I didn't want a happy middle. I wanted Chase forever. I wanted him until the very end, but he was leaving. He was agreeing that we needed space and if I wasn't going to fight, and he wasn't going to fight, then we were truly finished.

"It's the middle that counts," he affirmed, stepping forward and wrapping me in a hug.

My cheek hit his chest and I closed my eyes, gripping the back of his shirt so he couldn't leave. I inhaled the scent of him and tried to memorize how warm it felt to stand there in his arms. I wanted to cling to him forever, to beg him to be my hero, but my lips wouldn't move. I was paralyzed by the end of us.

"I have to go make lunch for my dad, but I left something on your bed that I think you should look at. It doesn't have to be today, but you need to look at it soon," he said.

I nodded and he stepped away like he was ripping off a bandaid. In one step, he stripped me of his warmth and from that moment forward, we weren't Chase *and* Lilah. We were Chase and Lilah.

I stood on the porch as he headed for his truck. The air swirled with remnants of his body wash and I told myself he'd come back and fight for us. I told myself we weren't over, but he disappeared around the corner of the house and a few minutes later I heard his truck rumble out of the driveway. I thought I'd crack, and maybe I did, but I still dropped that basket of vegetables on the porch and bolted upstairs.

I needed to know what he'd left me.

CHAPTER FIFTY-EIGHT

Chase

A SMALL PART of me feared Lilah would never come back to me, but I didn't have a choice. She needed space, and I was giving her that. I had to let her go with the hope that one day she'd come to realize that for her, I was home. We'd break out of Blackwater and start fresh somewhere without bad memories weighing us down.

I gave her space and I survived each day the same way a soldier survives war: keeping my head down and clinging to better times. As I changed my dad's bandages, I thought of Lilah in her garden. As I cooked my dad dinner, I daydreamed of sleeping with her out in the abandoned field. As I drove him to and from his hospital appointments, I resisted the urge to drive down her street to check if she was home.

"Do you want to stop at the store on the way home?" I asked as I helped him into my truck after the doctor had casted his arm. They'd had to wait for the swelling to go down before doing so.

"Nah, not today," he said with a groan as he adjusted in his seat.

My brows shot up in surprise. My father hadn't had a sip to drink since the day of the accident almost two weeks earlier. He was on some pretty strong medications and the doctors had warned him about mixing alcohol with them. To make it easier on him, I'd tossed all the alcohol that was in the house, but he'd taken his last round of pain pills the night before. If he wanted to, he could go right back to the bottle.

"How about we run through DQ and get a Blizzard?" he asked.

I couldn't remember the last time my dad and I had done something as simple as drive through a fast food place. I nodded and headed for the DQ just down the road. We each ordered an Oreo Blizzard and ate them while sitting in the DQ parking lot, with birds chirping and light filtering in through the back window of the truck.

It was the best afternoon I'd had with my dad in two years.

CHAPTER FIFTY-NINE

Lilah

CHASE HAD SET an old gardening book on the edge of my bed. Its pages were yellow-tinted and the binding was torn. I sat down on top of my comforter and pulled it closer so I could inspect the front cover. It claimed to be an encyclopedia of plants that could grow well in Texas.

I gently tugged open the front cover and froze when I saw my mom's scribbled handwriting right next to mine. We'd each signed our names.

This book belongs to:

Elaine and Lilah Calloway

My letters were nearly impossible to read, but I could make out the "Lil" in Lilah. I ran my hand over the old ink and then turned to the next page. "Fruit Trees" was printed in bold across the top and beneath that my mother had scribbled a few notes. I oriented the book and held it up just below my face so I could read her writing better. The light from my window poured over the page, illuminating a forgotten piece of my past.

This morning I asked Lilah what type of fruit trees she'd like to grow. She listed grapes, oranges, and bananas—probably because they were still on her mind after breakfast. I explained that grapes grow on vines and that banana trees take up a lot of space. Then she said she'd rather do raspberries anyway, so we're going to try raspberries this year. I doubt Lilah will let them ripen long enough before she picks them. Raspberries are her favorite right now.

I didn't realize I was crying until a tear traced down my cheek and fell onto the page. The fat drop of water sat directly next to her writing and I simultaneously wiped it away with one hand and reached with the other hand to block another tear from ruining her penmanship.

I'd had no clue the book even existed. I realized it must have been hidden in those boxes of her old things—things I had no interest in looking through, but Chase had. He'd found something I never would have.

That first page was as far as I got that day, but it was the start of a change. When I closed the cover and took a deep breath, I could almost remember scribbling my name alongside hers.

CHAPTER SIXTY

Chase

"I CAN'T BELIEVE Trent got kicked out for the rest of the year," Brian said, letting his tray slam onto the lunch table hard enough to tip over my bottle of water.

I reached up to right it before it spilled onto my tray. "He did?" I asked.

Brian nodded.

"He's in juvie for a few months and then he has to repeat his second semester to graduate," Brian said, twisting off the cap to his Gatorade.

"Where'd you hear that?" I asked.

"I overheard the ladies in the front office talking about it while I was waiting to see the college counselor," he explained.

"He deserves even more than that," I said with a sharp

277

tone. The police had questioned me and Ashley a few times after the event, but I hadn't been sure what they'd do to Trent. Guess I finally had my answer.

Connor walked up to our table and slid into the seat beside Brian.

"If we don't beat Oak Hill this week, we're officially out of the playoffs," Connor said as he took a seat.

"Thank you for that reminder," Brian groaned, tossing a fry at him.

I was half-listening to their conversation, half-wondering where Lilah was. For the last two weeks she'd switched back and forth between eating lunch in the library and eating out in the nature center. I always angled myself toward the front of the cafeteria on the off chance she'd walk by. A few times, I'd spotted her with her mother's book in her arms, clutched close to her chest. She'd texted me the night after she'd found it, just a simple thank you, but I knew it'd meant something to her.

I gulped down some water and then glanced up to the entrance of the cafeteria where windows spanned from the floor to the ceiling. I spotted Lilah walking through a small crowd of students with her mom's book in her hand. She seemed intent on heading for the school doors, which meant she was going to the nature center that day.

"Dude. Stop stalking her and focus. I just called your name like four times," Connor said, throwing a French fry in my direction. I shot him a warning glare. I'd been an ass lately, but there was really no way around it. With everything going on, I was lucky to get through the day without blowing up on somebody.

"I'm listening," I said, resisting the urge to look back at Lilah.

She'd switched groups in physics, which meant those

fleeting moments of spotting her around school were the only thing I had to sustain me while I waited for her.

"We were just talking about renting a spaceship and flying to the moon after school."

"Sounds good," I said as I tried to catch one last glimpse of her before she disappeared outside.

"Dude! I knew you weren't listening."

I flinched as a handful of fries hit me in the face.

• • •

Later that night I walked into my house after practice, sore and tired. I needed to shower, cook some kind of dinner for my dad, and then finish my homework. Finals were coming up and my AP tests loomed.

I sat my bag down by the door and then straightened up as I caught of a whiff of something in the air. *Garlic.*

"Dad?" I called out as I walked down our main hallway toward the kitchen. The light was on, and as I got closer I could hear pots and pans shuffling around on the stove. When I turned the corner into the kitchen, I paused. My father was standing at the stove with headphones on, mixing some kind of sauce.

I couldn't remember the last time I'd seen him cook.

I walked up and patted his shoulder so he'd know I was there. He turned and pulled out one of the headphones.

"Oh, hey, I wasn't expecting you back for a little while. I would have had this finished already," he said, gesturing to the food.

"No worries, I still need to shower."

He nodded, shifting his eyes back to the chicken. "Okay, well yeah, the food will be ready when you're done."

"Do you need any help?" I offered, pointing to his casted arm. He seemed to have managed just fine so far, but I didn't want him to push himself too much.

He glanced down at his arm with a frown and then shook his head. "I've got it."

I nodded slowly, assessing the stove once more before turning and heading up to shower. I felt like I was in the twilight zone. My dad hadn't touched a bottle in two and a half weeks, he was keeping the house clean, cooking dinner, and earlier that morning as I'd left for school, I'd heard him on the phone with a customer from the repair shop.

I tried not to think too much into it. Instead, I took the stairs two at a time and focused on everything I had to get done for school.

CHAPTER SIXTY-ONE

Lilah

I TOOK A small bite of my salad, feeling my dad's stare boring into the side of my head.

"Do I have something on my face?" I asked, sliding my gaze to him. We were eating dinner by ourselves that night and it felt weird without Chase there.

My dad's brows shot up, and he shook his head before taking a bite of his turkey sandwich. *Nice try.*

"You're not going to tell me?" I asked.

He narrowed his eyes on his sandwich and then shrugged. "For the past few weeks, you've been quiet like you used to be when Chase first moved in."

I thought about his observation for a moment, wondering if he was right. "It's a different kind of quiet."

"Oh really? How so?" he asked with a small smile.

I picked at my sandwich. "I'm not sad like I was then. I'm just..." I paused, trying to clear up my thoughts. "Figuring a few things out."

He chewed his bite before asking, "About Chase?"

I shrugged.

"You know, I really like the kid. It's more fun with him in the house, and I didn't want to admit it, but he makes better pancakes than me."

I smiled. "Even if we started dating again, he wouldn't move back in. He's taking care of his dad," I pointed out.

He frowned. "True. Do whatever you want then."

I laughed.

"He's in love with you though. You know that, right?"

I nodded, eyeing my food. I knew.

"All right, all right. I'll change the subject. How do you want to celebrate your birthday next week?"

"I haven't really thought about it."

Every year my birthday marked the end of spring. Growing up I had loved the idea of being a spring baby. After all, spring was supposed to be *my* season. My mother had named me Lilah Rose to commemorate that fact. When I was young, I'd count down the days to my birthday with mixed feelings. I'd want the cake and the presents, but I didn't want the season to end.

However, for the last two years, my birthday had served as a reminder that I've survived another spring, that the struggle would soon end.

"Can I take a rain check?" I asked with a simple smile.

My dad furrowed his brows, clearly wanting to push the subject, but I knew he wouldn't.

After dinner, he went into his room to watch game footage, and I pulled my mother's book out of my backpack and flipped to where I'd slipped my bookmark between the worn pages earlier that day. I'd left off at the beginning of the vegetable section, and before I started reading, I went out onto the back porch and sat on the top stair. Reading her scribbles and working in my garden always brought me a sort of solace, so combining them meant that my breaths came easy and my thoughts smoothed themselves out.

As usual, her handwriting gave me a jolt of nostalgia as I read over the first few lines of text.

Lilah insisted we start planting the vegetables early. We normally plant seedlings, but this year, she wants to do seeds. We'll be trying zucchini, squash, and bell peppers. Maybe next year we'll plant even more, but I didn't want to get in over our heads. Chris built a few raised beds out of some old lumber so Lilah and I would have somewhere to plant our seeds.

Her words overflowed into the margins and I had to turn the book to read them. I wished I could have asked her why she chose to write in a gardening book instead of a journal. She could have filled entire pages with her words, but instead she was confined to the small spaces left over in the margins.

Upon finding her gardening book a few weeks earlier, I'd searched through the rest of her things, hoping to find a journal, but there was nothing else lurking in the boxes. The small gardening book was my final connection with her. At once, I craved to read it all, to greedily rush through every word, and yet, I wanted to savor it slowly and make it last forever. It felt like for those brief moments I had my mother back, the real one who'd been there for the first seven years of my life.

Lilah and I figured out that yellow squash tend to need a bit more water than the zucchinis.

I ran over the text a few times before slipping the

bookmark back between the pages and standing up to grab the garden hose. I headed straight to the squash, where the vines were growing wild and big yellow flowers were starting to sprout. I let the water soak into the dark soil, giving the plants extra water just as the book instructed, all the while feeling closer to my mom than I had in ten years.

CHAPTER SIXTY-TWO

Lilah

I STOPPED BY Crosby's Market on the way back from school the next day. I walked through the aisles and paused in front of the display of hair dye. My roots were in bad shape and I couldn't ignore them any longer.

I stared at the smiling woman on the front of the box of blonde dye. I'd resented her months before, annoyed with her easy smile. Now I didn't think she was so bad. Even still, I reached for the box of black dye, not because I had an agenda or because I wanted to be a rebel.

Nope, I just liked the black.

I hurried the dye in my hand as I walked the mile to Ashley's house. It was starting to warm up and by the time I reached her front door, I was practically melting. Summer had almost arrived.

Ashley opened the door after I knocked and I held up the box of dye. "Can you spare a few minutes for a friend?"

She scanned over my blonde roots and smiled. "I thought you'd never ask."

CHAPTER SIXTY-THREE

Lilah

I'D BEEN OBSESSED with uncovering the secrets and lies of Blackwater, Texas because I had a theory I desperately needed to prove: no one was as happy, as perfect, or as good as they were pretending to be.

For half of my childhood, my mother had been the subject of every whisper uttered in my small town.

She was the bad mom who'd left her daughter.

She was the drug addict who couldn't get clean.

She was the lost woman with no hope of redemption.

I watched everyone in my small town turn against her, pulling back inch by inch until she was nothing more than a shadow they tried their best to avoid. They'd pull their children back when they saw her approaching, they'd cross the street and avert eye contact. I watched them judge her and dissect her choices, confident that they were better, they were wiser, they were happier. Superior.

I was confused by the hypocrisy of it even as a kid and now I had a journal that proved my theory.

We all tell lies. We all live in delusions.

So why was my mom so terrible? Why were her failures not met with forgiveness?

Because her lies were on the outside. They were written across her face, plain to see. They were uncomfortable and dark and big enough that they made other lies seem small and simple. Infidelity, fraud, gossip were all eclipsed by my mother's crashing and burning.

Her failures made everyone look better. Everyone could be a great mom, wife, or friend if only they compared themselves to Elaine Calloway.

A part of me wanted to spread the truth I knew. It'd be so easy to scan the pages of my journal and print out a thousand copies. Our town was small and an afternoon at the copy shop and a couple of rolls of tape was all it would take to coat it in cold, hard truth. I wanted everyone to realize their mistakes, to feel the sting of embarrassment they'd forced my mother to feel, but I never could pull the trigger. Maybe because I knew firsthand that every person in that town would have to face their own truth sooner or later, or maybe because in my gut, I knew my desire for vengeance was dwindling more and more each day.

I carried two books everywhere I went during the end of that spring semester: my mom's gardening book and the journal I'd filled with secrets and lies. They seemed to go hand in hand at first. I'd skim through them both, finding solace in the worn pages, but then one day, I skipped over my journal.

My mother's words were like a salve on my heart,

patching up the wounds I'd tried hard to cover up. Eventually I knew I wouldn't need the journal any more, not if I really wanted to move on.

The secrets and lies of Blackwater weren't my concern. Not any more.

CHAPTER SIXTY-FOUR

Chase

OUR FIRST PLAYOFF game was scheduled for noon on Saturday. I held out no hope of beating our opponent, the reigning state champs, but I'd play my best and keep my head up high as we walked off the field. For most of my teammates, it'd be their last baseball game, but I had years of college ball left.

I was set to start and as I warmed up on the mound, the blazing sun scorched the skin on the back of my neck. I reared back, drew my leg up off the ground, and hurled a curveball at Connor. The ball collided with his glove with a sharp pop. I lived for that sound.

Conner stood, straightened his catcher's helmet, and tossed the ball back to me. I caught it and moved back to take my position for another. I glanced up into the stands to find the Diamonds Girls in their seats, their matching shirts a dead giveaway. Parents and fans surrounded them, but I didn't see Lilah's short black hair anywhere, and if she wasn't there, then I didn't care who was in the stands.

I finished three more warm-up throws before the announcer spoke through the field's scratchy speakers.

"Welcome to the 3A Region 2 playoffs! We have the defending state champs, the Lake Johnson Rattlers taking on the Blackwater Wolves. Starting for Lake Johnson we have…"

The announcer's voice carried on but I tuned him out as I lined up next to my teammates.

I'd just made it to the front of the line when two figures walking up the middle aisle of the stadium caught my attention. Lilah and my dad were walking up the ramp side by side. He was carrying a bag of peanuts and she had two sodas. She pointed to two open seats at the front of the bleachers and they slid past other fans to take their seats. When he turned, he scanned the field and then found me, staring up at him.

My throat tightened as he smiled and waved. It was a small, self-conscious wave; he was nervous about being there and I had no way to reassure him other than to smile, take my hat off, and wave back.

I couldn't believe it.

My dad could change.

·

CHAPTER SIXTY-FIVE

Lilah

I FINISHED MY mother's book the night before my eighteenth birthday. It was dark out, nearly midnight, and I lay in my bed illuminated by the soft glow from my bedside lamp. I'd thought I liked to garden because it was something I did with my mom. It was a passion we shared, and most of my happy memories with her took place in the garden.

But that's not why I continued to garden after she died.

I gardened because I was obsessed with the notion of finding beauty in the dirt. Dirt is chaos, gritty, full of bugs and decay, but from that dirt comes such immense beauty. Roses, tulips, tomatoes, peonies, raspberries, oranges, magnolias...and even me. I wanted to be made new. I wanted a fresh start. I wanted to take my past, with its sadness and torn edges, and turn it into something beautiful and worthwhile.

I'd been chasing spring ever since my mom had left me when I was seven. For eleven years, I'd poured my soul into my garden, planting and cultivating, thinking that if I made the garden beautiful and full of life, it would fill me with beauty and life in return.

But I was wrong.

In the end, spring sprung from the pages of an old book.

At the very end of my mother's book, there was a page a little more crinkled than the rest, a little more worn and forgotten. On it, I found this:

I don't know what next year will bring, but this spring has been about us, Lilah and me. We've spent every afternoon out in the garden and she's loved every second of it. As I write this, she's tugging on my hair, wanting me to finish up. We're off to pick our raspberries from the vine and she's so excited. We've waited patiently for them all spring and finally, they're ripe.

I closed the book and rested my hand against the front cover, trying to process everything at once. The value of the journal was in the details. Her messy handwriting had illuminated something for me that I'd never thought I'd understand: my mother loved me the only way she'd known how. She'd loved me fiercely and now I had tangible proof of it.

In the end, that's all that I could ask for. Her love was different from other mothers' love, but that's the thing about life. We have grand visions of our lives because we assume we are the center of the universe while in reality, the universe doesn't even realize we're there.

New mothers are made every day, most with tears of joy in their eyes. I think my mother's were tears of sadness, not because she didn't want me, but because she knew she couldn't be the type of mother that a daughter needs.

She'd done the best she could, and as I let her gardening book fall onto my chest with a soft thump, I felt wholeheartedly content in a way I hadn't since the day she'd left.

I took a deep breath, a breath that cleansed my spirit, and then I reached for my computer to pull up a map.

CHAPTER SIXTY-SIX

Chase

I'D JUST SETTLED into bed with Harvey at my feet when I heard a tap on my window. It was quiet, hardly there at all, but a second later, there was another tap, and then a third.

I pushed up out of bed and padded toward the window. I pulled the blinds up to find Lilah standing in the flowerbed in front of my window, armed and ready to throw more pebbles.

When she saw me, she loosened her fist and dropped the unused rocks.

"What are you doing?" I asked, pushing the window up a few inches.

"Let's go," she said, waving me out of my house. No explanation, no please.

I turned to look at the clock on my bedside table: 11:45

PM.

"It's late."

She made a show of rolling her eyes and then propped her hands up on her hips.

"Chase. C'mon! We have fifteen minutes until my birthday starts."

"Hold on," I relented, scanning over her. She was wearing jean shorts and a tank top. Wherever we were going, it wasn't fancy.

"Psst. Bring Harvey too!" she called after I'd turned away from the window.

Harvey was already scratching at the door.

Five minutes later, I crept out my front door with Harvey at my heels. My dad was a heavy sleeper, but our door's hinges were ancient and I swore as I swung it closed it could have woken the dead. I froze for a few seconds, listening to see if I'd woken him up. *Nothing*.

I was in the clear.

I turned to find Lilah behind the wheel of her dad's truck, waiting for me to join her. She looked the same. Same cropped black hair. Same fuck-all attitude. Same green eyes that reminded me of every important moment of my life.

"Did I make it in time?" I asked, opening the door so Harvey could hop in.

"Nine minutes," she said, tapping the dashboard clock.

"Nine minutes left of seventeen-year-old hell," I said, sliding in beside her.

"Nine minutes left of being stuck in this small town."

She started the car and pulled away from the curb.

"Nine minutes left until you can buy cigarettes," I offered.

"Nine minutes left until I can buy all the cigarettes I can

carry and light them on fire," she responded.

I laughed.

"Are you going to tell me where we're going?"

She scrunched her nose. "No. That's not fun."

I shrugged and stared out the window. The street lamps did a poor job of lighting our path, but Lilah seemed to know where she was going.

Harvey curled up into a ball between us as we started our drive away from Blackwater. An hour passed, then two. I wanted to ask where she was driving, but I never did.

"Thanks for giving me time," she said a few hours into our drive.

We'd gone a month without speaking and then out of blue, she'd arrived outside my window, no apologies, no explanation.

Sometimes life is too short for explanations.

"Did your read the book?" I asked.

She gripped the steering wheel with both hands and nodded. "Every page."

"And?"

"And here I am."

Her hand dropped from the steering wheel to Harvey. Her palm was an open invitation, and I reached out to take it. Just like that, I knew she was mine for good. There was no going back now.

"A part of me thought you'd never be ready to come back."

She nodded, scanning out over the road. "I worried about that too."

We drove for miles, slipping between small towns without much notice. We stopped for gas and food around 2:00 AM. She grabbed two coffees and I grabbed an armful of candy and chips—road trip supplements. The gas station attendant eyed us with curiosity when we dropped our loot on the counter, but he withheld his questions. Did we look like two teenagers running from a small town? Was that what we were doing?

When we got back to the car, I pulled out a Hostess cupcake and stuck a half-eaten Twizzler into the center of it like a candle.

"Happy birthday, Lilah," I said, holding it out for her.

She smiled and then squeezed her eyes closed to make a wish.

"Quick," I joked. "Before the wax drips."

She opened her eyes, met mine, and leaned forward to blow out the Twizzler.

After four hours and two bags of peanut M&Ms, I fell asleep for a while, lulled by the white noise of the freeway. When I woke up sometime later, we were driving over a bridge, surrounded by water on both sides.

Lilah's green eyes slid to me. "We're almost there."

I sat up in my seat and glanced around us, trying to place where we were. Thousands of islands sit off the coast of Texas and we could have been driving onto any one of them.

We continued on through a sleepy beach town. The shops were all closed except for a Starbucks on the corner of Main Street. As we passed a donut shop on the corner, their neon "OPEN" sign turned on. Light was just beginning to pierce the black sky as we pulled into a parking lot across from a beach covered in shadows. Seaweed was scattered across the sand, laying in clumps where the tide had come in overnight.

"We almost didn't catch it in time," Lilah said, opening her door.

"Catch what?"

She glanced back at me and smiled. "The sunrise."

I let Harvey out first and he took off down the beach, his blond fur lit up in the dawn light. He chased off seagulls and dove headfirst into the waves. We walked to meet him and he came running back toward us, already a sandy mess.

"Do you recognize where we are now?" Lilah asked, stepping around the car and reaching her hand out for mine. I laced my fingers through hers and shook my head.

"Galveston?"

It was the first Texas beach that come to mind.

She smiled and shook her head. "Port Aransas."

My stomach dipped as I stared back out over the beach, trying to pick up on any familiar landmarks. There was sand, and ocean, and seaweed, nothing that gave away the fact that I'd been there before. It didn't seem any more special than any other beach, and yet, it was.

The last time I'd been there, my mom had been alive. The last time I'd jumped in those waves, my mom had held my hand. The last time I'd touched that sand, my mom had been standing beside me. She'd stood right where I was, letting her feet sink into the sand the same way mine did.

"I wanted to come here for my birthday," Lilah said.

"Why?" I asked, staring out beyond the horizon.

"Because being here with you and your mom is the last perfect day I can remember," she said, squeezing my hand for assurance.

I nodded, letting her words sink in as the sun started to creep up over the horizon.

"I think this is the start of mine."

~~THE END~~
THE BEGINNING

R.S. Grey

ACKNOWLEDGEMENTS

I have to take a moment to thank my husband Lance. He was as much an author of this book as I was. He helped me rewrite at least five different versions and over a dozen drafts. Over the last two and a half years, we reworked this story together.

After a publisher passed up the chance to publish this book last year, I took a step back and worked on other projects, all the while wondering whether or not Chase and Lilah deserved to see the light of day. In the end, it was Lance who convinced me to pursue this story the way I wanted to write it. I am so proud of this book and I hope you enjoyed reading it as much as I enjoyed writing it.

All my love,
Rachel

Made in the USA
San Bernardino, CA
10 August 2016